The Secret Life of Birds and Bees

By: Tinker Jeffries

Dedications

I never thought I would be an author; God pointed me in the direction to open my own lane and succeed as I determined to make a path through. First, I want to give thanks to the loyal readers that stuck by my side; reading my blogs since 2011. Your positive feedback pushed me to grow as an author and motivated me to take authorism seriously. When I published my first novel in 2013 "Sex Symbol Stories Vol 1" you supported me and purchased a ton of books. I'm very thankful for the love. I want to say thanks to my fiancée Tiffany for accepting my dirty past and riding by my side even though the people of our surrounding judge and tried to bring us down because the literature I write. I love you to death, I can't see myself without you. I can't wait to give you my last name. Hey, Mom (Wave Hands) Even though you don't approve in the erotic novels you were the first person that bought my book. Thanks for raising two boys by yourself in a single woman household. Mr. Darrell was a blessing as well when stepped in our life. He filled in the blanks to assist you raise great men. Thank you as well Mr. Darrell. Shout to my kids Iyonna, Peyton, Darren Jr, Dallas and Bryce I love all of you with all my heart. My Dad Darren Hardy, You're a great man and an awesome father. Mama I love you, you're such a sweet person. Devon, Braylon, sweet pea, Jasmine and Dae Dae I love everyone of ya'll.   Thanks to the editor and publisher Chardaé you definitely came through in clutch time also, I want to thank Rochelle Mullins for the graphic design.

001. CAN'T DISPOSE GOLD

SHAYLIN
Friday

Keys jiggle on the opposite side of the door.

It's Friday night ten minutes to midnight I glimpse at the time on my pink Apple Watch. I've been laying comfortably on the couch in my night gown with no panties on, scrolling through my Instagram feed barely paying attention to what's on the television. After a lengthy twelve-hour work shift at the hospital as a RN and a hot steamy shower; relaxation is exactly what I require desperately. It's been a long-lasting slow dragging week. The only thing on my agenda this weekend is to unwind, watch my shows on the DVR and maybe get some dick. Quickly my Instagram scrolling is interrupted as the door slowly opens.

"Hey, babe." Steve greets me twinkling his gorgeous dimples as he smiles while holding shopping bags in both hands.

"Hey." I pause for a second to glimpse down at my watch to reassure the time. I was more astonished at the time he came home than what he had in the bags.

"You're home mighty early." I utter, acting surprised as he swiftly makes his way towards me still lugging the bags over and then planting a kiss on my forehead before he sat beside me.

Handsome that's an understatement Steve is more fascinating to the eyes than that. I met him four years ago outside of a restaurant called The Original and still remember it like it was yesterday. The Original is a diner at Pitt University campus that everyone attends after the club for late night greasy foods. The drug dealers and men with their fancy cars hang out across the street with their gold chains and designer clothing, leaning on the hood with their music booming; stunting for the ladies dressed in their attention seeking short dresses and fuck me now high heel pumps.

That night I was with my friends Tasha, Brittany, and hoe ass Alisha when I heard a deep voice speak into my ear from behind me while I was stuffing French Fries in my mouth.

"Can I have some?" he asked, I glared back slowly with a "what the fuck" expression written all over my face" not amused and writing him off as a lame before I even looked his way. That was until I caught eyes with this beautiful stranger. A French Fry sloppily fell out my mouth, hitting the concrete in snail motion as I swallowed my potatoes in one big gulp and eyes wide. This man was about 5'11 chocolate with two sleeves full of tattoos, he had freshly twisted dreads, nice full lips along with white perfect teeth and his eyes would have any woman on earth fall into a daze of love. I'm not hoe ass Alisha but at that moment he could've got the ass the minute our eyes locked because my pussy was screaming for this man. He wore a white slim V-neck t-shirt exposing his muscles in his arms and his baby gut, short gold chains around his neck that had diamonds dancing on the face of Jesus. Black Slim fit Levi jeans hugged his 34-inch waist accessorizing with a Louis Vuitton belt and wallet hanging from his belt loop.

"Yes, you can." I answered his question politely as held the brown bag of fries towards him to offer. "Nah, I'm good." He said shooting me a smile that almost made me pass out as I pulled the greasy bag of fries back towards me then he went on. "You're very attractive, what is your name may I ask?"
I forgotten my name for a second then Alisha hoe ass answered, reminding me what my name was. "Her name is Shaylin and I'm Alisha." She introduced us with hints of flirty swimming in her tone. I shot Alisha a neck-breaking glance, my eyes squinted with rage of flames to warn her hoe ass to sit down and be humble before she got a severe ass whooping in front of all these people. She turned her head quickly knowing for sure she didn't want no mishaps.

"Shaylin, my name is Shaylin." I glared back at Alisha as I repeated my name.

"I'm Steve everybody calls me Prince." His eyes went from my eyes then glued to the Pittsburgh Police cars strolling in a slow pace down the street. I followed his glare and then looked over at him.

"Are you okay?" I questioned. He snapped out of what thoughts he had cluttering his mind then brought his attention back to me.

"Yea… Yea… I'm cool." He nervously replied.

I despised calling people by their nicknames for the reason it makes me feel less important, his hoes he claimed not to have at the time can call him that. "I'm going to call you Steve."

We exchanged numbers and that day is where it all started. It's funny how a simple "Hi" or in my case "Can I have some fries?" can lead to a couple. For the first year, our relationship was amazing we were beaming and our love for one other was unbreakable. Extraordinary vacations in and out the country, sensational conventions day and night and mind-blowing sex, which hasn't left. Our bond was like no other we were so happy.

After the year passed I completed school and earned my Bachelor's, we moved in together and rented a plush two-bedroom apartment on the East End. All in the mix we were blessed with a healthy son who is now eighteen months. When the honeymoon stage was over the shit hit the fan and literally splattered all over the damn walls. We were arguing day and night, there were days he wouldn't come home, his time for me was interrupted by his other love; the streets and these nasty whores. For the past couple years, I thought Steve only owned a cleaning business but it was more than that. When I was cleaning the house, I discovered two bricks that looked like white blocks in the corner of the closet in our bedroom wrapped in plastic. Mom always warned, "You don't know someone until you're under the same roof."

…

He reaches in the Nordstrom bag excited as if it's Christmas or something and I just stare indifferently. "Here I got something for you." He pulls a creamy white Louis Vuitton Bag out then hands it to me.

"Thank you, baby." I say forcing excitement to escape my lips. He was always good for bringing home gifts after a heated argument and after last night I'm skeptical.

"Look in the bag." He shoots me that smile I fell deeply in love with when I first met him.
I reach in my new designer bag and retrieve a little red box. My stomach fills with butterflies and at the same time my heart drops to my knees especially when Steve slid off the couch then kneels on to his knees. My hateful feelings towards Steve quickly goes to "I love the fuck out of this man" in a finger snap. I'm so deep in my emotions, my eyes fill up with a bucket full of tears as I nervously tremble trying to open the box.

"Open it." He voices with delight.

I open the box slowly, my eyes became wider from the bling of the humongous diamond on the platinum ring, I place my free hand over my mouth with disbelief as I soak this moment in like a sponge.

"Can you marry me Shaylin, I'm sorry about that shit I said to you yesterday. I just want you to know I love you to death, I want to grow old with you. So, can I be your husband?" he softly spoke with sincerity pouring from his voice.

"Ye.. Yes... baby!" I say leaning towards him to hug him.

When our bodies separate, he stands to his feet sits beside me.

"Where's Lil Steve?" He glances back over his shoulder towards Baby Steve's Bedroom.

I rub his thigh gently. "He's at my mom's house, I dropped him off before I came home." Without a doubt, I'm giving my man some sweet pussy tonight.

"Oh huh." Steve strokes his goatee looking like he's in deep thought. He reaches for his belt buckle then zips the zipper down to expose his grey boxer briefs.

"Suck my dick." He demands firmly in the time he recline back on the sofa. That's all he has to say. Without a word, I rapidly drop to me knees; face in between his thighs. When Steve takes authority, it turns me the fuck on! His manly command causes my pussy to pulsate and my juices to flow like Niagara

Falls. I massage his dick outside his boxer briefs, in seconds his manhood grows to full attention.

"Daddy getting hard I see." I say in a kiddy tone, glaring at Steve seductively.

He nods his head to show agreement. I pull his boxers down and his dick leaps out like an actor at a haunted house. His black dick is standing strong with healthy veins bulging out his thick nine inches. My mouth waters like it's a juicy steak sitting in front of me and I haven't ate in days. I grab hold of his hardness then slither my tongue across the cone. I remove his pants fully from his legs then continue to give him my best.

He looks at me with ecstasy in his eyes motivating me to continue. "Umm..." He starts, as I sloppily drool all over his shaft, licking up and down with fervor. I feel his legs go rigid as my tongue trails down to his balls, his moans grow louder.

"Umm... damn baby." He wails in pleasure.

I grasp his solid black handle; stroke it while I suck his balls like a Hoover as I glide my tongue in unison. His eyes are closed and his head tilts back with gratification while enjoying my oral skill set. "Damn baby, ohhh shit ohh shit," he moans. Four years of being with Steve I have complete knowledge in how to give pleasure to my man sexually. There isn't nothing like someone who knows how to give you the best sexual intercourse or orally please you the way you like to take pleasure. I separate my mouth from his balls with saliva drizzling heavy down my chin as I lift my head up to wrap my mouth around his dick. In the time, I continue to stroke his manly pole then began to bob my head all in one rhythm; stroking and sucking. I'm moaning enjoying myself as well while I'm performing both simultaneously. Seconds into me sucking his dick he places his hand over top of my skull, pushing my head down with force as he penetrates my mouth causing my throat to travel balls deep.

"Suck this dick, suck this fucking dick!" He demands as tears of joy form in my eyes.

Not even a minute later I felt his shaft of his dick get extremely hard.

"I'm about to cum, I'm about to cum," he announces mumbling as his legs tighten. "Keep going, keep going!" At this time, I was sucking the fucking skin off his dick, my head bobbing up and down like a rubber bouncy ball.

"Yes, yes baby, yess…" His body balled up like notebook paper formed into a paper ball as his cum flew out his dick like a speeding bullet to the back of my throat. His chest heaves up and down attempting to catch his breath as he glares at me with heart eyes. Mouth full off cum I stood to my feet then turn to make a dash toward the bathroom, before I can take my first step he grasps my wrist glaring directly in his eyes.

"No swallow that shit and sit on this dick." I glance down at his dick, surprised it was still standing strong, hard as fuck; I close my eyes shut then swallow his juices.

Wet is an understatement my pussy is wetter than the water slides at Kalahari Water Park, I lift the night gown above my waist then slowly slide down on his dick, sitting face to face. Chills shoot through me body as his thickness fills me up. "Oww!" I wail in the time I slide down every single inch of his dick while he spread my ass cheeks apart.

Gradually in a mild pace I bounce on him with my arms wrapped around his neck, the sound of my wetness made squashy noises like someone was shaking a half of bottle of water. He consistently thrusts up as I come down on his manhood; teamwork makes the sex more amusing.

"Yes daddy, yes give me that dick give me that dick." The more I moan the harder he digs inside of me. His chest heaving in and out against my size 34 B breast; my man gives me his all and so do I.

Swiftly we change positions, I lay flatly on my stomach across the couch, he props his body over top of mines with one foot on the floor then shoves his rod deeply inside my pussy. Using his hips, he throws powered stokes consistently hitting my spot causing me to scream from the bottom of my lungs.

"Yes… oh yes… daddy… yes… give me that dick!"

He lays his hand over top of my head then aggressively drives my face into the seat cushion like he's striving to make sinkhole in the couch with my features.

"I'm about to cum daddy, I'm about to cum."
He is fucking my fucking brains out!

"I'm cumming." My moans grew so loud it could've broke a glass vase.
After making love in the living room we go another round in the bedroom. A couple orgasms later, we are out of breath yet begging to fill the silence on account of what just happened.

"Love you baby." He plants kisses on my forehead in the time I relax my head on his tatted chest.

"Love you too. You really can see yourself only being with me for the rest of your life?"

"Yes, can you?" he fires back the question after his response in low voice.
I glare up to look in his eyes to firmly assure him I was ready for him to be my husband.

"On Monday can you deposit the money in the envelope I left on the table?"

"Okay, I'll do that before lunch."
Not even five minutes later we both shut our eyes then drift off to sleep happily engaged.
...

"Ring... Ring... Ring..."
Steve's phone in the living room rudely wakes me out of my slumber and I scowl towards the cable box.
"3:16 AM" the time read in white lettering. Slowly I turn my attention to Steve catching all the z's with his mouth wide open snoring like a baby without a worry

in the world. At a slow pace, I slide out the bed then tip toe my way out the bedroom avoiding to make the wooden floor squeak. Prior to stepping out the bedroom the phone rings again I stop in my tracks as my heart drops to my bare feet.

"Shit," I mouth as I glimpse back to catch a sight of Steve still in deep sleep.

Heart beating like a drumroll as I curiously grasp his phone, I couldn't believe my eyes. I read the message three time as I stand there in disbelief. Tears form in my eyes as I read every word. I snap a photo of the messages with my phone beside his. I storm my way into the bedroom with his phone and my phone in hand then shove his shoulder hard as fuck. "Steve!" My tears fall heavily on the bed.

"What... What babe." He says in a groggy voice.

I should've put his phone in his face. "WHO THE FUCK IS THIS BITCH!" I sob uncontrollably with tears cascading down my face. The longer I stood there the more my heart was breaking into a million pieces it would take more than glue to repair it back together. He rubs his eyes with both hands acting confused

"Huh?" He says now acting like he's confused.

"WHO THE FUCK IS A!" I repeat then I read the text out loud. "BABE. I THOUHT U WAS COMIN OVA TONITE, I MIS DAT DIC!"

"THAT BITCH CAN'T EVEN WRITE IS THAT WHAT YOU WANT! STEVE!"

When Steve finally decides to sit up shit goes all the way bad.

...

JAY
Monday

"20, 40, 60, 80, 100 here you go Ms. Smith" I slide the cash under the glass window to the elderly olive colored woman. It's the third of the month and the bank is packed wall to wall like we're giving out free money.

"Thanks, young man." The old lady shot me a smile flashing her perfect white dentures while retrieving her currencies.

"You have a good one Ms. Smith" I shot the lady a smile back then I attend to the next customer.

"Welcome to Citizens Bank how may assist you?" I say in my best businessman impression as I smile and wiggle my blue tie.

This is my second week working as a bank teller at Citizens Bank in the East Liberty branch on the east end of Pittsburgh. When the judge slammed the hammer on my older brother Owe; sentencing him five years in the state prison for burglary in the third degree, I instantly changed routes and straightened my path.

I was a professional thief; we were breaking into mansions in the wealthy communities swiping items that had a nice price tag. We stole jewelry, cash, guns and whatever had value. This one time I stole a million-dollar painting and sold the artwork for three hundred thousand dollars which I divided in three ways with Owe and my cousin Juju. The money was coming faster than speeding bullets, our lifestyle transformed from normal young adults without two pennies to rub together to living lavish. We were on top of the world enjoying expensive jewelry, designer fabrics, plush two-bedroom condos on the North Shore with a beautiful view of the city's skyline, luxury cars and stunning trips out the country.

The women! Shit the women were attracted to me like magnets. Other than my habitual thieving addiction I was a junkie when it came to the ladies. I damn near laid down a different broad in my bed every single night up until I met this attractive woman Amber at Original's four years ago, in the middle of Pitt University. Owe, Juju and I was sitting at the table throwing down on our late-night snacks; I was devouring my breaded shrimp and basket full of fries; which I probably wouldn't eat sober. Everything is pleasurable to the taste buds when you're under the influence of drugs and alcohol; when I say drugs, I meant that lime green marijuana.
Original's was crowed shoulder to shoulder, there were two long lines with people desperate to order their food, all chairs at each table were occupied. The

place sounded like a million people were talking in unison. I was minding my business biting into a hand full of fries after dipping the potatoes in the mix bowl of cheese and ketchup when I noticed the most eye-appealing woman I ever laid eyes on standing in line staring me down. Amber, had a long blond ponytail that swayed down to the middle of her back, at this time she was in her mid-twenties with a smooth brown sugar complexion. She wore big gold hoop earrings, shiny lip gloss that highlighted her full beautiful lips, tight light color blue jeans that exposed her phat ass and a blue jean short sleeved button up shirt which was buttoned half way which had her cleavage bulging out. I scanned her body from head to toe impressed that she had some of the prettiest feet I ever saw as she wore the fuck out of her red bottom pumps. She flashed me a smile and waved flirtatiously. I sent a smile back showing all thirty-two teeth as I felt Owe's beefy forearm gently settle on my shoulder, he leaned towards me in a brotherly manner, bringing his lips near my ear.

"Damn bra you see shorty, she choosing. You better swerve on that." He spoke softly practically whispering.
"Umm Humm," I nodded my head with agreement as I chewed my food gazing directly at Amber with the *I want you* grin on my mug. Juju's eyebrows shot up with puzzle written on his face

"Who the fuck is you two eyeballing?" He took a glimpse back over his shoulder, following my gaze then quickly darted his eyes at Owe then me.

"Ayo, Jay that bitch is bad as fuck," he said blaring with excitement as he leaned forward from the opposite side of the table, damn near stretching his neck to where Owe and I sat.

"Ju, calm your horny ass damn fam." I uttered in a stern low voice giving him the stink eye.

Juju braced his lips, glanced over his shoulder for a second peep then he spoke again as he turned his attention back towards me.

"Her friend will get it too." In the time Juju spotted his prey a lanky beige guy about six feet with a sandy brown crispy temple fade, displaying True Religion fabrics and Jordan sneakers sloppily approached Amber.

"CAN YOU LEAVE ME ALONE!" Amber's words stood out over every conversation held in the restaurant, her pretty face was full of disgust as she shoved him on the chest. Amber's little push didn't make the beige guy budge; he swatted her hand and pushed closer up on her invading her personal space.

"GET THE FUCK OFF ME!" She nudged him again, this time a little harder.

 Each second that ticked as I watched this coward ass nigga disrespect Amber the hotter I became. Out of frustration I tapped my left foot against the floor. I didn't have to voice one word Owe and Juju glared at me already knowing what on mental.

"Tap, tap, tap, tap" until I had enough.

"GET OFF HER!" Amber's friend intervened to rescue her BFF.

I drove both feet into the floor causing the metal bottoms of the chair to make a loud annoying sound as it slid back.

"BITCH YOU GOING PLAY ME AFTER I TOOK YOU ON A TRIP TO JAMAICA, I SPENT ALL THAT FUCKING MONEY ON YOU!" I heard the guy utter with anger in his tone, probably spitting in Amber's face. Surprisingly I strolled toward the three calmly like there's not a worry in the world, like Donald Trump wasn't the president.

I stood beside Amber, gently planted a kiss on her left cheek then put my right arm around her shoulder. She glanced at me as if I was her knight in shining armor, just like that her defense was replaced with relief. I looked directly in the guy's red eyes. "Look fam, this is my girl. I don't know about the problems y'all had in the past but now she's my problem." I said politely even though I was steaming like a teapot deep inside, one sign of disrespect and I was capable to blow like a whistle. The people in our surroundings of the restaurant cut their conversation short and watched us like a Love & Hip Hop episode. They were probably hoping for shit to escalate. His nose flared, chest expanded then he pointed his index towards Amber.

"THAT BITC…"

I stopped him mid-sentence. "What I say fam? She my problem now I advise you to get the stepping or we going have problems." This time I spoke with fire in my tone. He stepped back with the quickness scared shitless.

"Okay, Okay, I'll leave." He inched back with his hands up in surrender.
Stepping near the door he finished his sentence. "That bitch is a money hungry hoe!" he said then disappeared out the back door.

After a few dates, she became my woman; our relationship was one of the romantic relationships that you would read about in books. I didn't mind sharing my wealth with her she was my everything. It's not tricking if that's your woman. There's people out here with all the money in the world with no one to love who are miserable as shit. As long as the bills were paid and I was breaking into houses I didn't give a fuck about what I spent on my woman, it wasn't like she stayed home and didn't work. She had a job at the post office at that.

…

Now that I'm an employee for the bank and no longer breaking into houses; our relationship got real rocky. As I sit here behind the glass window smiling, behind this perfect smile of mines was darkness.

"I would like to deposit this money in my business account." A beautiful brown freckled face queen with pretty brown round dreamy eyes says as she slides an envelope under the slot of the window.

The color of her long wavy hair is a darkish red, her eyebrows are perfectly arched looking natural, she has full wet lips and a small diamond in her nose. She dressed in a baby blue scrub with a stethoscope around her neck." I read her nametag clipped to her chest

Shadyside Hospital RN, Shaylin Stewart

I retrieve the stacks of cash from the envelope "What's your account number?" I ask as I notice the big diamond ring gleaming on the ring finger.

"I don't know the business account numbers but I have my ID." She glances down in her creamy white Louis Vuitton bag then fished around until she retrieves her driver's license.

She slides the Pennsylvania identification card towards me. I take a peep at the photo on the card then take a quick glimpse at Mrs. Shaylin Stewart; my eyebrows go up and my lips clamp tight as I admire her beauty. My pace obviously annoyed her because I can see the agitation in her face.

"What? That's me. You think I'd give you a fake ID." She says with sarcasm in her tone after huffing with exasperation.

"No, No, No" I plead shaking my head. "I'm just admiring your picture on your driver's license, your very photogenic."

Her frustration quickly turns into a slight smile. "You look as good as you look in person." I shoot a compliment as I swiftly type the ID numbers on the card into the computer to pull the account number. There were two names on the High-Quality Cleaning Service account, Steve Johnson and Shaylin Stewart. I put the money in a money machine and let the apparatus count the dollars to the amount that was given to me in the envelope. I place the bills in the drawer then present a receipt with the total that's in the account.

"Thank you. And thanks for the compliment. I just been going through some things nothing against you." She says with a smile that seems like it hurt.

"Shit, I understand." I nod my head with comprehension, the situation at home had me feeling abnormal as well. "Well I hope… I mean, everything going get well, we got to speak shit into existence."

"Yeah, you're right." She concurs.

"Hey." I speak with hesitance as she turns to walk away.

"Humm?" her eyebrows rise.

"If you don't mind, I would like to have lunch with you one of these days." I utter not even thinking about my significant other.

"I don't know if I can take your offer on that, I'm engaged but you're cute though." She turns then disappears out the door.

Sitting on the hard-uncomfortable chair in the breakroom I already used ten minutes of my thirty-minute lunch break heating up the leftovers from my

Uncle Peter's cookout in the dirty sauce stained microwave.

"Oh, shit, Oh shit" I say watching these two drunk country white boys fight like animals in a cage over a beer. The fat red neck with tattoos in a red flannel cut sleeve shirt connects his fist firmly against the skinny bearded man causing him to dramatically stumble to the ground. Worldstarhiphop.com is definitely entertainment in my free time. As I scroll hoping to come across another video on the site just as amusing as the last video, my phone rang, **"Babe"** displays on the caller ID with Amber's picture I captured on the beach in Fiji.

"What's up babe." I answer with dryness in my voice still bothered from last night.

"Hey baby, how's your day?" she asks in happy high pitch tone.

"It's Good, How about you, How's your day?" I adjust myself in the hard chair.

"It's fine, I just went a little shopping. Did you think about what we talked about last night?"

I knew she was going to bring the conversation up from last night. Instantly she gets under my skin. "No, I haven't, I'm not getting myself into that shit. Especially not
 with some niggas I don't know! how many times I'm going tell you Amber!" I growl.

"I'm just asking dang..." her happiness tone went flat really quickly.

"Look I have a J O B Now Amber! You're going have to respect my decision." I take the last bite of the macaroni cheese that my grandma Joy made, wishing I had more.

"Okay, baby I respect your decision but this is an opportunity to make lots of money, you wouldn't have to work for no white man ever again. You can be a boss like you use to be."

Her words hit me like brass knuckles. "I'm not about to have this conversation." I stand firmly, she has me so fucking hot I could just throw my phone at the wall.

"Babe, Babe can I…" Midsentence I press the red end button on the phone to end the call.

…

"Ding," the elevator stops on the fifth floor, the mouthwatering whiff of pasta has my taste buds dancing as I stroll through the hallway to my apartment. It must've been Ms. Marino the old Italian lady in apartment 516 cooking dinner. I sure wish I could be sitting in her dining room digging in some of her saucy Italian flavors. When I slid the key in the key hole, I notice the smell was coming from under the cracks of my door. Instantly I began to get suspicious as I turn the key and push the door open to be met with a dark living room with candles burning on the end tables.

What the fuck is Amber up to? I think as the aroma slowly moves my legs to the dining room. The table in the dining room is dressed like a five-star restaurant, there is a humongous block of lasagna with a thin curl of smoke lazily arising as the cheese melted onto the clear glass plate, beside the plate next to another is the fork and the knife along with a tall glass of wine. Amber is glaring at me seductively under the relaxing brownish orange candle flame that stands in the middle of the table. My eyes scan her body from head down to her polished pink pretty toes with desire as she sits at the table alone waiting for me barely dressed, wearing a thin black see through bra exposing her nipples and thong set revealing her sexy brown super model legs. My watering mouth now was watering for her juices, at this moment my feelings about greed were erased completely. I just wanted to sweep everything off the table including the steaming hot food then aggressively fuck her on top of it. The power of the P U S S Y drastically alters my suspiciousness to a straight up horn ball, it's insane how I was on the verge of ending this relationship and beginning a new life without Amber but now I'm second guessing. She won me with her sex appeal.

"Take a seat babe." She speaks with sexiness flowing in her voice. At a leisurely pace, I take a few steps then sat down across from Amber.

"I prepared your favorite dish." She adjusts her body in the chair to face forwards.

 "Thanks baby, What's all this for?" My eyes wander the table.

"Because I appreciate you. You've been an outstanding man since we met, no matter if you take the job with Larry or not I'll stand by your side no matter what the circumstances are." Her words were like a massage on the back.

"I appreciate you too babe. This lasagna looks delicious can we eat now?" I ask jokingly as I rub my hands together glaring at the plate as if I was ready to attack.

I stick my fork in the last bit of the flavorful lasagna then wipe my mouth with the napkin, despite the headaches Amber gave me in the past month I can confess she can throw down in the kitchen.

"Only if you knew how much I love your cooking." I utter smiling while I shake my head.

She slightly giggles as she stood to her two feet.

"You say that every time I cook for you." She says reaching in front of me to retrieve my greasy empty plate.

"That shows you that I'm not lying." I gaze at her ass switching in the time she makes her way to the kitchen.

"Well I have something else for you to eat that's more luscious than dinner. You can call this the Amber's special dessert. Go in the bedroom and take off all your clothes."

I hear the plates clanking in the sink as the water pours out the faucet. Promptly my dick grows hard; revealing a crease of my nine inches in my straight fit suit pants, her words has my hormones jumping like a pogo stick. Without a doubt, I stand up and walk to the bedroom calm, cool and collective. Best believe I could run in there and rip my clothes off like a man turning into a werewolf when there's a full moon. I strip down to my birthday suit, sit on the bed, and patiently wait for Amber's debut appearance in the bedroom. The candles are lit on the two nightstands and the orange lights from outside leak through the cracks of the blinds, I hear police sirens somewhere in a great distance in the neighborhood. In minutes my thoughts are interrupted by a knock at the door.

"Knock, knock, knock"

"Who is it?" I glare at the door playing Amber's little kiddy knock knock game.

"It's me cutie with the booty."
She knocks again

"Yo, who's at my fucking door?" I ask jokingly as I slowly stroke the rim of my hard-black manhood.

"Daddy if you want this sweet treat you better open this door."

I slide off the bed, stroll to the door then turn the knob. Instantly she drops to her knees with a can of whipped cream in hand. She sprays the cone of my dick then slides the tip of her tongue across it. I gaze in her eyes as she takes a look in mine with deep affection. Amber lifts the can up; spraying my shaft making a foam line that matches my every inch then she slithers her tongue up and down my pole slowly as whipped cream and saliva trickle down her chin.

"Damn, Babe damn babe." moans slip out my mouth. She grasps a hold of my handle, wraps her pretty lips around my dick then began to take me in something seriously. With a combination of consistent strokes and neck motions my knees feel like noodles heating up in hot pot of water. She's sucking my dick like there was no tomorrow or next week. Her signature ponytail swings side to side while she inhales and exhales my length and thickness, her oral talents feel so damn pleasing it forces me to ponder why I can't withdraw from this relationship. I honestly don't want other niggas to experience her sexual, love making, make a man bust a hard nut expertise. Mid stroke, she put an end to the amazing head she was throwing me which compels me to glance down. Amber bites her bottom lip with rapture in her eyes as my dick pulsates severely springing up and down.

"Your turn." She stands to her feet with the can of whipped cream in hand, with her free hand she grasps my hand then escorts me to the bed. She laid on her back, spread her legs open with her feet resting on the edge of the bed as I stood in front of her glaring down between her thighs while she massages her clit through the thin material of the thong.

"Time for Amber's special." she speaks slowly sliding off her underwear. Once she fully removed her thong, she tosses it at my chest. In the time the thong falls to the carpet floor she aims the white tip of the Reddi Whip then sprays her clit like a juicy strawberry.

"Come eat your dessert."

She doesn't have to speak twice I kneel to my knees, grasp hold of her thighs, gradually pull her body towards me then smash my face in the pussy like cake at a wedding when the bride and groom cut the first slice. Even with a messy whip creamed facial I clamp my creamy lips around her clit then slide my slippery tongue across it back and forward as I fill my mouth up with saliva.

"Oh my gosh daddy, Oh my gosh." She sobs as she places her hand over top of my head. "YES, YES eat this pussy!" she encourages me. "It's yours baby, it's yours, it feels so fucking good!" she pushes the back of my cranium down some more adding force like she was attempting to shove my head inside her pussy. I continue to slide my tongue against her clit and tenderly suck as my fingertips massage the ridged ceiling of her G-Spot in unison.

"Yes baby, yes!" her moans grow louder and louder, I know for sure the neighbors below hear Amber's shrieking. Shit, it won't surprise me if the neighbors beneath them can hear her as well.

"Oh shit, oh shit, oh shi..." her legs depart from the bed like 747 jet and hang in the air as she pushes down hard on my head.

"Here it comes, here it comes" she warns me. That was always my cue to remain steady and focus on frequently hitting her spot because if my lips move one bit or if I stop stroking her with my arched fingers that would be like pressing the restart button on an orgasm. It was like building a house then knocking it down with a bulldozer, right when the last finishing touch is painting the walls. I keep licking, sucking and sliding my fingers in and out.

"I'm cumming, I'm cumming!" By the third time she announces it another time, her legs stiffen, and hands detach from the back of my head. Both of Amber's hands randomly wander the bed to retrieve something else to grasp on which was a fist full of sheets in one hand and the edge of the mattress in the other as she releases a coating of ecstasy all over my lips.

"Shittttt," She wails. I keep sucking and licking even after she comes.

"Oh, shit stop, stop, stop" She pleads crawling back as she shoves her palms against my forehead to remove my lips from her goodies, probably because her pearl is sensitive from the breathtaking orgasm.

She lay there quivering in an orgasmic shock as her chest heaves in and out while breathing massively. I honestly don't want to blow my own horn, but I ate the fuck out of her pussy, she probably was in a whole another world.

I don't give her time to recuperate, swiftly I wipe the sweet juices off my chin then yank her body toward mine by the thighs; Aggressively dragging her to the edge of the bed. I plant my feet firmly to the floor, grasp hold of my already hard manhood then plug it gradually inside of her warm ocean, her barrier of pleaser tightens as I shovel deeply.

"Ummm." She moans with her eyes shut as I thrust out then thrust back in constantly.

For the introductory, I stroke her at a slow yet firm pace.

"Oh, damn baby I can feel that dick in my stomach." She utters in a sexy moan. The momentum of my down tempo penetrating speed as she moans from each and every stroke. I ease my grasp from her throat then I turn towards Amber to meet for a kiss. The kiss was actually passionate for the first time in a mouth of Sundays. Our tongues tied with ardor like shoelaces on new Nikes in unison as I penetrate her insides.

"Yes, Yes, Baby!" she wraps her legs around my lower back and swaddled her arms around my neck. Amber's sex is always amazing, but this night amazing is an understatement. There's not one word that I can register in my mind how mind blowing our love making is.

We fucked like two wild animals, each stroke I land she pulls herself into my thrust.

"I want you to cum with me, I want you to cum on this dick." I groan pumping my waist with rhythm between her legs as sweat beads form on my forehead.

"I... love... you... I... Love... this...fuck...ing...dick." She speaks each word between strokes.

In and out, in and out our naked bodies collide making skin clapping noises blended with headboard banging against the wall and our moans. In no time, I feel a wave of chillness shoot from my toes to the standing hair on my neck.

"I'm cumming. I'm... about... to... cum.." She moans each word separately.

"Cum with me, cum with me" I demand in a shaky voice.

"Ughhhhhhhh" I groan but this time much louder as my body gets frail. Simultaneously she screams.

"Oh, my goshhhhh." As she unravels, her arms tighten around my neck. At that split second, our wetness clashes with one another as we both cum at the same time.

After we fuck for another hour we lay next to one another. I'm well on my way to sleep as she watches Snapchat videos.

"Babe." She speaks so relaxed with honey in her tone.

"What's up babe?" I turn my focus toward Amber hoping to God she doesn't mention something about running up in someone's house.

"Can... I have $1,500," she boldly asks. I go from half sleep to fully awake in no time. I have a few thousand saved, but that shit is for emergencies.

"For, What?" I ask glaring at her like she had three eyes.

"Because, I need it."

"What you need it for, that's a good bit of money." I scratch my head with confusion.

"I...I... need it to book a plane ticket with my friends, we're going to Miami next month."

"Your plane ticket is $1,500 what are y'all taking a jet?" I give her a half giggle "I'll think about it; I'll have to sleep on that because my funds are getting low."

She turns her body the opposite way then distance herself away from me. "You wouldn't have to think about nothing if you went on that job with Larry." She whispers under her breath loud enough to make sure I could hear.

Those words are like uppercuts to the chin from Floyd Mayweather "WHAT! WHAT THE FUCK YOU MUMMBLE UNDER YOUR BREATH!" I bark sitting up glancing down at the back of her head. She doesn't utter a word and her silence has my blood boiling even more. "IF I WENT ON THAT JOB WITH LARRY. HUH? IS THAT WHAT YOU SAID? You know what. Now I'm not giving you shit."

She whips her head in my direction with rage written all over her beautiful face. "YES, I SAID THAT SHIT!" She yanks the sheets from over her body "I CAN'T DEAL WITH NO BROKE ASS NIGGA. I TRIED TO

34

HELP YOUR BROKE ASS MAKE SOME EASY MONEY
BUT SINCE YOU DON'T WANT THE JOB, NOW I HAVE
TO SUFFER." She catches her breath then rolls off the
bed to stand to her feet. "I GUESS I'LL HAVE TO GET
THE MONEY SOMEWHERE ELSE. IT'S CRAZY HOW..."

"IT'S CRAZY HOW WHAT!" I Interrupt her in
the middle of her furious rant then finish the
sentence "YOU CAN BE OUT HERE HOING! GO BE
WITH THEM NIGGAS I'M TIRED OF YOU THOWING
THAT SHIT IN MY FACE!" I yell outraged with thunder
in my tone. Amber's silhouette stands in the doorway
as the dim kitchen stove light shines behind her; chest
heaves in and out as she huffs and puffs. She doesn't
like the hoe statement; this is my first time
downgrading this woman out of the four years we
dated. The apartment fills with silence the only noises
I hear now are from the motor running in the fridge
making a buzzing sound.

"You know what Jay, that's just want I'm going
to do." She whispers through grunted teeth. "Maybe
I'll find a nigga that can treat me like a lady like you
once did."

For a minute, I second guess my remarks, I
honestly hated to watch this woman leave my
presence and I sure can't imagine another man dick
dipping inside my Amber epically after I invested so
much into to her like money, trust, respect, love and
most importantly my time that I will never get back; I
wish I can get a refund for all that shit. My regretful
thoughts vanish rapidly when she speaks again.

"Maybe I can fuck with Larry. That nigga is a boss. Unlike someone I know." She smirks knowing what buttons to press. That's what it took to cement the end of our relationship. I was so heated if water was thrown on me the liquid will convert into steam. I swiftly stand to my feet bare naked, dick swinging and all, deep down I want to smack the fuck out of this bitch but I witnessed my mother take brutal beatings given by my step father in my youth, so putting my hands on a woman wasn't an option. Instead I glare in her eyes with my eyes lowered filled with pain behind them.

"GET THE FUCK OUT MY HOUSE! PACK YOUR FUCKING SHIT. YOU UNGREATFUL BITCH." I yell in a beastly growl. And just like that she packs all her clothes then disappears into the hallway after slamming the front door with these last words.

"You're going to regret this."
….

(Two weeks later- Citizen's Bank.)

It's Monday morning and the doors are unlocked for customers to come in to handle their finances. I'm behind the glass window replacing a roll of paper in the receipt printer

"How go your weekend Jay?" My co-worker Anna Lee a beautiful Asian woman in her mid-thirties asks in broken English as she counts a stack of ones.

"It was Okay. I did a little drinking and hanging out you?" I respond struggling to close the printer.

"Whoa sounds fun Jay. I didn't even get no sex; my weekend was boring Jay. Boring."

Shit I didn't either, I thought as the roll of receipt paper popped out the printer then made its way on the floor.

"FUCK!" I utter.

"Excuse me ma'am you, have to take your glasses off." I hear Kevin, the lanky white security guard demand in a shaky voice in the time I bent to retrieve the roll of paper. When I stood up to observe the commotion, the guard had his arms stretched out attempting to block the lady with the sunglasses from coming further inside.

"Move out my way. I have to withdraw some money!" She shoves his arms out the way and storms past him. I shot a quick glance at Anna, her rosy colored skin goes yellow. She was spooked like the lady was going to rob the place. If a genie could grant Anna one wish I guarantee she'd wish to vanish from this bank.

The guard is on her tail as she walks to the middle table where the deposit and withdraw slips are. "Ma'am I'm going to tell you one more time to take those sunglasses off they're not permitted inside this bank." He's beyond irritated I can tell by the wrinkle on his forehead. I gaze at the woman again; her hair was a hot mess like she just woke up out the bed and said "fuck It," then went about her day, she was dressed in a black hoodie with black tight jeans the exposed that fatty she was dragging behind her but she appears to be very familiar.

"And I'm going to tell you one more time sir, NO!" she yells glaring dead in his face then she grabs a slip and a pen. I turn to Anna who was now panicky - that's an understatement she is on the verge of shitting on herself, her hand creeps under the cash register to press the alert button. Before she can hit the button, my memory button was pushed. The crazy lady was Shaylin the nurse from Shadyside hospital, something was wrong for her to be so jumpy and distraught.

"Anna Please don't push that button, I know her." I dart from the back then enter the lobby. The guard yanks Shaylin's arm aggressively then she goes off like a siren.

"GET OFF ME YOU RENT-A- COP," She pulls her arm from his grip.

I hurry towards the two before shit escalates even more. "Hey, Kev I got this man. I know this young lady. She my long-time friend." I glare at her with a grin on my face. Kevin backs off at the same time they gaze at each other like worst enemies.

"So," I adjust my tie "May I help you with anything" I ask. I notice her hand is naked; she isn't rocking that humongous diamond she flashed two weeks ago. Sunglasses on a rainy day and no engagement ring, when I put two and two together then it hits me like some brass knuckles; Her dude is abusive.

I ask Shaylin once again to take her on a date after assisting her financial needs, sliding her $2,000 all in hundreds; a repeat of last time she declines my offer but fortunately, she takes my number.

...

SHAYLIN
Shaylin Mother's house. Two days later.

It's been two weeks since I read the disturbing text message that broke my heart into little tiny pieces in Steve's phone. I'm certain he has hoes stored in his black flip phone along with the drug users that calls him for their next hit. Those bitches in his trap phone aren't relevant but when a man gives his personal phone number to a woman that signifies she's more significant which shows he cares for this bitch. I rudely wake him out his sleep confronting him about a bitch in his phone he stored as A. I'm positive the home wrecker bitch name began with A and for days I ponder all the A names I can think of like I was attempting to name a newborn baby with the first letter of the alphabet. I bitch and curse a storm regarding to the woman he's creeping with, but Steve was too pussy to man up and confess. Instead, he leaps off the bed with murder written on his face. A mass of fear shot through my body, which causes me to step back. Swiftly I dart out the bedroom, through the dining room to the front door in the living room. Steve is on my trail the whole way though and as soon as I touch the doorknob I felt his hand grasp the back of my neck.

"YOU FAT BITCH I TOLD YOU, I DON'T KNOW WHO THE FUCK SHE IS." his strong hands around my throat tightly. His comment referring to my weight hurt more than his tight grip. Tears fall down my eyes as he went on. "I TOLD YOU, YOURE NOBODY WITHOUT ME. AIN'T NO NIGGA GOING TO WANT YOUR FAT ASS!"

After giving birth to my son I gained a few pounds and developed a slight gut with Tiger strips across which are called stretch marks, Steve couldn't stand my striped stomach. There were nights he wouldn't touch with me unless I had a shirt on.

I reached for my neck to make an effort to put a gap between my windpipe and his hand as I struggled to breathe.

"WHAT YOU GOING DO LEAVE ME!" He compressed his grip like vice grip.

"HUH! HUH! YOU GOING TO LEAVE ME BITCH HUH!" each Huh he hostilely jerked my neck with force.

I couldn't utter one word; he was strangling the fuck out of me as if he was seeking to end my life. When he let loose of my neck he stormed to the bedroom for a hot second, retuned back to the Livingroom with an arm full of my clothes.

"If you want to leave then bitch leave." He said in a low scary tone. Steve tossed the clothes at my chest, I caught one or two items but the rest sloppily tumbled to the floor.

"You won't be needing this either." He threw my phone at the wall like a major-league baseball pitcher causing my iPhone 6 to shatter.

"Now get the fuck out." He growled.

My son and I stayed over my mother's house for the weekend by Sunday night I returned home after his apologetic call on the cordless house phone. He bought me the latest iPhone and some new red bottom heels; the gifts weren't nothing compared to the father and son bond the two boys had when they were together. That's when I realized that I willing to work out whatever to keep my family together.
A week later Steve left his phone face down in the SUV cup holder, plug in the changer when he disappeared in the convenience corner store while I sat in the passenger seat. I was scrolling through The Shade Room, a popular blog account on Instagram, reading the daily tea on the celebrities as I double tapped a photo of Quavo from Migos at the BET awards. Steve's phone rang. I glared in the store to perceive if Steve was coming out, he was somewhere in the store hiding behind a shelf full of goodies. My conscience told me to ignore the ringing phone but my woman intuition informed me differently my eyes darted to the glass window of the store to his phone. He was nowhere in sight

"Fuck it!" I said under my breath with a heart beating like a drumroll. Hesitantly I reached for the ringing phone when I caught sight of the name stored his phone instantly I began to tremble with hurt and rage. My woman intuition never stood me wrong it was that mistress bitch A. With unsteady wobbly weak hands, I pressed the green accept option to answer the phone.

"Hello." I said in a calm tone deep inside I was fucking screaming.

"Well, Hello is Prince there." Her voice flowed through the other end of the phone with condescending in her tone.

"This is his fiancée may I ask who this is?" I stretched the word fiancée to let that bitch know who the fuck I was. She let out a slight giggle.

"You don't need to know all of that. Put our man on the phone." Instantly I snapped like fingers, I could've just snatched the bitch through the phone and beat her ass to a pulp.

"WHAT YOU SAY BITCH, OUR WHAT!" I spat flames

"Our man, where is he at?" still speaking in a calm snobbish tone, that shit got me even more mad.

"LOOK BITCH YOUR GONE GET!"

Out of nowhere I heard the driver's door open. "Ayo, give me my phone." Steve ordered as he sat down to reach for the cellular device. I denied his request and pulled my right arm back so the phone can be out of his reach.

"WHO THE FUCK IS A? STEVE!" I said with tears forming in my eyes. The only words that he can utter were

"Give me my phone." He leaned over to attempt to retrieve his phone but now we were tussling

"GIVE ME MY FUCKING PHONE BITCH." He said in a booming tone as I waved the phone back and forward in the air to reject his strive. The Bitch A probably remained on the phone getting a kick out altercation she was hearing.

"WHY STEVE? WHY? YOU SAID YOU WERE DONE WITH THAT BITCH!" I sobbed, face raining with tears.

"GIVE ME MY FUCKING PHONE YOU FAT BITCH." That's when I felt his fist strike me in the left eye. I released the grip of his phone like it became hotter then lava rocks then suddenly I tended to my eye that was puffing up rapidly. I placed both hands on my face and cried and cried until I had the courage to lift my head up.

"I'm done Steve, I can't do this anymore." I opened the door and walked away. He followed me in his Range Rover beside my every step.

"Let's talk about this babe." He pleaded from the passenger window leaning over the armrest while another car trailed behind him patiently.

"NO! Please leave me the fuck alone, I'm done Steve." With tears still rolling down my face.

"Babe, I'm sorry. Get in and let's talk about it." His sorry ass continued to beg with sincerity in his voice.

"Beep beep." The driver behind quickly was losing their patience and so was Steve.

"GET THE FUCK IN THE CAR NOW SHAYLIN!" He spat in the time the dark skin guy's facial expression went from relaxed to annoyed as he pressed heavy on the horn.

"MOVE THE FUCK OUT THE WAY!" the guy yelled in unison as the horn continued to blow.

"I'm fine, I'm just going call me an Uber I'm done." I carried on walking.

"Oh! You're done." He paused for a slight second as the car behind him sped around Steve." "Okay, don't come back home and I want that fucking ring back." Without saying a word, I slid the engagement ring off my finger then threw that shit over his SUV to the opposite curb.

"Fetch that shit." I said then I sped my walking pace into a slight run. He slammed his brakes causing the tires to squeal.

"FUCK YOU, YOU FAT BITCH." He screamed as I heard the door open then shut firmly.

I ran and never peered back; once I located a safe spot to squirrel away I got an Uber ride to my mother's house and since than that's where I've been the past two days.

Earlier today this Monday morning at the bank I modeled my designer sunglasses but this time I didn't put them on for fashion; sad to say I had them on to shield the embarrassing swollen black and blue eye. I was striving to be low key as possible I didn't want people to stare and be judgmental, but the rent-a-cop had to blow my spot up with his reeking breath. The guard got under my skin following me throughout the bank, attempting to block me from handling business.

"Take your glasses off." He repeated maybe a million times which was pushing my button contently. I was seconds from getting possession of my pepper spray and showering his face until the beautiful rich chocolate bank teller intervened with his fitted white dress shirt accessorizing with navy blue tie, dressed in khaki slim pants and brown dress shoes. My heart melted like ice cream on a hot high humid day, when I mention chocolate, to tell the truth his skin looks like a brownie coming fresh out the oven. I would bite right into him. Two weeks ago, I had the identical thoughts regrading this man but two weeks ago I was newly engaged. He was around 5'10 in between mid-shinny and stocky, spectacular smile added with dimples and a thick beard. This man also smelled amazing, at that moment I had a desire to sniff his whole damn body. Us women have knowledge in who we want to give our pussy to, honestly, I would've fucked this man right in the bank earlier.

His name is Jay Reed, last time we encountered I denied his date request unfortunately he asked again but nevertheless I declined his offer again. I was stuck in the darkness of my last relationship, right then and now wasn't the best time to get involved with someone else.

`"That's fine." He said as he grasped a business card that has his first and last name on the front along with the bank name and his job title. He flipped the card then scribbled his number on the back.

"If you want to talk I'm here to listen. Since I can't get a date out of you." He shot me a smile then slid the card under the glass window.

11:39 PM at mother's house I'm in the guest room lying in the comfortable bed beside my son that's sleeping like there's not a worry in the world. This room used to be my bedroom back in my youth age, surprisingly my mother kept the cutout magazine pages of the young Bow Wow and B2K along with a handful of other artists taped on the wall. As soon as I began to reminisce on how amazing life was as a child growing up in Highland Park an East Side community of Pittsburgh my thoughts were interrupted by my phone chirping to inform me that there was a new message. I reached over my son slowly to retrieve the phone trying my best to avoid waking him up. Once the phone was in hand I read the text.

Babe. I'm sorry I need you to come back. Steve pleaded for the thousandth time. This man was soaking in his regret but this was a repeat episode. Each and every time he did something wrong he'd beg until his knees bled. I'm over the bullshit I mentally made a firm decision that I'm done for good, he didn't deserve a loyal woman and that's all that I've been for him. I was in his corner like a boxer's trainer no matter what the results was win or lose I was there. We're both iPhone users; yesterday I changed the text setting to inform him that the message was read under the message he sent. I ignored the message then suddenly the handsome bank teller clouded my mind so I reached over my son once again then grasped the business card with Jay's number on the back. The phone rang twice on the third ring I contemplated hanging up on the forth.

What are you doing? It's almost midnight he was probably sleep or occupied with a woman, I thought to myself.

"Hello." He said in a foggy voice, I can imagine him on the other end of the phone naked or maybe just in his boxers half sleeping wiping his eyes.

"Hey, it's me Shaylin the woman from the bank." I spoke hesitantly with shyness as I glared down at my son while he slightly shifted his body to turn his back towards me.

"Oh hey, hey, wow I didn't expect you to call me." Now the tone in his voice was filled with excitement.

"Sorry did I wake you up." I said with compassion.

"No, No you're fine how you doing?"

"I'm doing well." Deep down inside I wanted to mention that I was damaged I thought as I continued "Just lying in the bed next to my son. I should be sleep right now but for some apparent reason I can't."

"I know that exact restless feeling it was more like stress for the last couple weeks for me." Stress was less describing the shit I was feeling it was more like destruction.

"Well I guess we're in the same boat." I slightly giggled.

"I guess, but time will pass and whatever both of our situations are we're going look back be and be pleased in ourselves." His little pep talk had me about to scream "YAH"

We held a conversation for almost two hours; we literately poured all our feelings out the bag, he was like a best friend I never had. He listened to all my troubles and did not judge one bit. He mentioned his ex- girlfriend was a money hungry gold digger, she's now messing with a drug dealer and on top of that she had disappeared for two weeks. I guess we were really in the same boat just different stokes with dissimilar waves. Once the intriguing conversation got closer to the end, instead of him inquiring a date I asked."How about we have dinner Friday night?" "Sure. But dinner on me. A woman shouldn't pay on the first date." He said politely spilling his gentlemen rules through the receiver.

...

Friday Night

"Hey, love I'm outside."

I read Jay's text as I glared in the bathroom mirror at the healing eye, it was getting better each day. I applied makeup over the eye to cover up the black mark then I texted. "Okay, Give me one minute." Glancing in the mirror giving myself a double take before I flipped the light switch off to exit the bathroom. Despite the harsh words Steve used to break me down I thought highly of myself and tonight I was somebody to admire. I was dress in a shoulder less white dress fitting tight against my brown skin that stopped at the Leo lion tattoo on my upper thigh, black open toes stilettos pump that displayed my polished orange toes that Lee, the Asian guy painted at Al nail spa on Penn Avenue. Earlier in the day I got my hair washed, blow-dried and styled by Book Rae at 4ever L'amour Studio in the heart of Downtown Pittsburgh on Fourth Avenue. I accessorized with a cheap gold neckless that I thought was cute from Forever21 and a Rolex watch that Steve bought for my birthday two years ago. For the past week, you've would've thought I was zombie walking around with my head down with depression. That was not the fact tonight I was glowing feeling good about myself with pride in each step I took.

"Oh my God" My mother said with her hands to the mouth glaring at me with amazement, the same exact way she looked at me when I stepped out my bedroom with my prom dress on ten years ago.

"Look at you, you're so beautiful baby." She complimented me with a smile as baby Steve ran around my mother legs coming towards me with joy while swinging his teddy bear by the foot.

"Mommy, Mommy." He said in his jolly little voice with open arms, as soon as I extended mine he jumped in my arms to embrace me.

"Love you." I kissed him on the cheek.

"Love you too, Mommy." He replied then he continued "Where's daddy? I'm miss him." I glanced at my mother; she gave me a look of concern.

"Hey, pumpkin head let's get some snacks." She cut in on his thoughts.

He darted to my mother then jumped in her arms.

"Have a good time baby, be safe out there." My mother said with care then disappeared in the kitchen.

"You want some cookies." My mother uttered.

"Cookieeesssss." Baby Steve screamed with happiness.

When I opened the door, Jay was standing on the porch with a dozen beautiful red roses in his hands under the porch light. He was dressed in a short sleeve Lacrosse navy blue Polo shirt with the hat to match, brown fitted ankle dress pants and brown loafers.

"Wow. You're wow..." he stuttered with wide eyes attempting to let the words out his mouth. He gave me the roses.

"Wow. You're so beautiful." He shook his head. "I meant you're more than beautiful that's an understatement."

"Aww. Thank you. You're so sweet." I'm sure all the blood went straight to my cheeks as I blushed. Surprisingly when we approached his black Chevy Impala he reached for the latch on the passenger side and opened the door for me. He held the tip of my fingers as I sat down in his car.

"Thank you."

"You're welcome." He replied then shut the door. I eyeballed him the whole way around the hood of the car until he opened his door to take a seat. We haven't departed from the house and he's already spoiling me with royalty.

"Have you ate at the Hyde Park Steakhouse on the north shore?" he asked in the time it takes him to press the ignition button to start the car. Steve had taken me there one or two times in the past. Their juicy tender mouthwatering steak was definitely something to die for.

"Yes. I have, I love that place." I answered.

"Good, I made reservations for us."

JAY

Dinner Date

The candles were lit, and the vibe was beyond perfect. I felt like the most fortunate man in the restaurant. Upon noticing all eyes were on Shaylin I felt like the most fortunate man in the world. I happened to spot an elderly white woman smack the back of her husband's neck for staring a hole in my date's plump ass. I don't blame the man either if she wasn't in my possession and I was in his position I would've been the man catching a hot hand to the neck.

"So how long you been employed at Citizens?"

"About a month. This is actually my second job that I ever had." I said sipping the fine red wine as we patiently waited for the food we ordered minutes ago. The restaurant lights were dim, and the place was filled with people engaging in conversations.

"Really? Where did you work before the bank?" she asks. Telling her that I'm a former thief was out the question instead I falsified the answer, I scratched the side of my head thinking fast to utter a fib.

"Well my uncle had a buy and sell business. People would sell their gold scraps or electronics to us for a low price and we would sell them for a higher amount. Whenever he went to jail the business went downhill drastically. That's when I applied for Citizen's Bank. I had to attend three interviews and two weeks of class."

The waitress appeared with hot plates in hand with steam twirling off the steaks, instantly my taste buds began to dance.

"Mmmh that looks delicious." Shaylin said glaring at the food as the waitress placed the plate in front of her. She ordered the Steak a La Lobster the restaurant was famous for and it came with asparagus, béarnaise and sliced mushroom spread over top; for the side, she has Lobster Mac & Cheese. I opted for something similar to Shaylin's, but I had the garlic steak with mushrooms and garlic butter flowing over top, for the side dish roasted garlic whipped potatoes and salad.

"Is there anything else you two need?" The lady waitress said as she poured more water into Shaylin's half empty glass of water. The waitress darted her eyes at me, I shook my head from side to side

"No. No thank you."

Her eyes darted towards Shaylin who gave her a smile and the same answer. "Okay. Enjoy." The waitress said smiling then she disappeared towards the kitchen.

"Let's bless the food before we eat." Shaylin said as I stabbed my steak with the knife and fork. "Bow your head." She demanded.

I closed my eyes shut and bowed my head. The fact that she was a spiritual woman had me astonished, my father who's no longer alive always told me "A woman of the lord will make a stronger man."

"Lord thank you for this food that we're about to receive," in the middle of blessing the food my phone rudely rang. My reflex caused me to quickly reach for the phone in my pocket to silence the ring, I shot a brisk look a Shaylin with one eye open and one eye shut as she finished up the prayer. "Amen."

"Amen." I repeated after her as my phone rang again. I reached inside my pockets to grab my phone and that's when heart dropped to the floor. The caller ID the name read, *"Gold Digging whore."* I knew It was petty but I changed Amber's contact name to exactly what my perspective of her actions were three weeks ago. I ignored the call again, sat the phone on the table face down then turned my attention to the beautiful woman in front of me. She was devouring her food not paying me or my ringing phone no mind, that was somewhat of a turn on. I truly loved when a woman eats without being shy in front of a man, I despised when a woman picks at their food with that insecurity shit. I bet women like that will lick the plate clean when a man isn't present.

"When I first saw you in the bank for the first-time I instantly fell in love with you. I was like damn yo, I have to say something." I said smiling while I cut into the juicy meat.

She shot me a smile back. "I was surprised you even said something to me, I was looking rough that morning"

"Not in my eyes..." The damn phone rang again. I glared at Shaylin her face went immediately blank, irritated with the interruption.

"Are you going answer your phone? Apparently, it must be urgent if they're consistently calling you."

"No, it's nobody important." I brushed Shaylin's words off ignoring Amber's phone call. I turned the ringer off then sat the phone face down on the table and continued digging into my dinner. When I finished chewing I resumed to the previous topic before my phone rang.

"Like I said, not in my eyes…" The fucking phone rang again.

"I'm sorry, hold on one second." I asked her for one second placing my index finger up. "HELLO! WHY ARE YOU BLOWING UP MY DAMN PHONE!" I spat with annoyance streaming through my blood.

"Hey baby, how you been? I was calling because I was thinking we should make this work." Amber said calmly like she hasn't been missing damn near a month. Shaylin's eyes were glued on me and I'm sure her ears were too.

"Look Amber, I've moved on with my life. You had your chance, but you blew that when you couldn't respect the changes of my lifestyle. So please can you leave me the fuck alone and let me be like you have in the past three weeks?"

"Fuck you, you broke piece of shit." She yelled then ended the call.

After dinner, we took a stroll on the North Shore Riverside Trail to view the beautiful Pittsburgh city skyline. When I dropped her off the night ended with a goodbye kiss.

When I arrived home, it was 11:58 two minutes from midnight. To be honest after a long day of work and then an amazing date with Shaylin I was exhausted I couldn't wait to jump in my bed butt-ass-naked. The elevator seemed to move up floor to floor slower than usual. When I got to the third floor I let out a loud yawn, my body was giving me conformation that it was time to take my ass to bed. It seemed like forever before the elevator finally reached the fifth floor. Strolling sleepily down the hall my face twisted in confusion noticing a trail of clothes on the floor and what made it bad was it was all my clothes.

"What the fuck," I thought. My tiredness quickly turned into alertness. Slowly I tip toed down the hallway. I was nervous as a black man getting pulled over by the most prejudiced cop. Two doors away from my apartment I caught a glimpse that my door was wide open. Gradually with a rapid beating heart I stepped foot in my apartment to witness a catastrophe. You would've thought a tornado twirled through my place, the couch pillows were flipped, sliced open and the cotton in the couch was leaking like blood. The television was face down on the floor and the lamps on the coffee table were demolished. I hurried to the bedroom and the smell of bleach reeked as I walked in. The mirror to the dresser was

smashed and all the drawers were pulled out and emptied. On the top of my bed my clothes were spread on the bed and the strong odor of bleach hit me even harder. This bitch Amber was the first person to come to mind.

SHAYLIN

Monday Afternoon.

"Today kind of slow. We're trying to find a volunteer to go home early." The white mid 40-year-old nursing supervisor Kim Webb announced with a Dunkin' Donuts coffee cup in hand as she sat at the desk in front of the computer monitor. She was saying nothing but a word.

"Well, I'll volunteer I have a lot of running around to do anyways." I said slightly excited.

"Thanks. I really appreciate you Shaylin. My boss was on my case." She said then turned her attention back to the computer and began to type something. In minutes, I was out the door calling my man.

Last Friday the date with Jay was spectacular he's 100 percent all gentlemen I felt like a queen in a fairytale book when I was with him and at the end of the night when he kissed me I almost melted into a puddle. His kisses were so soft and passionate that I died twice went to heaven and then came back to Earth. The one thing that caught my attention that bothered me the most; he kept his phone face down. I'm not his significate other but that's a BIG sign with huge letters SNEAKY. We talked twice after the date he mentioned that his ex-girlfriend vandalized his apartment and poured bleach on his clothes. If I was that man I would be coming for her head, I would make her pay for all the damages.

Last night I received a call from Steve and for the first time in weeks I answered the phone. "Hello." I said in a soft tone while baby Steve watched Sponge Bob on the television at the end of the bed.

"Hey, baby. How you doing?" His sexy deep voice sent a shock wave through my body.

"I'm fine." I kept my answers short, even though I was ecstatic to hear his voice I still had to play hard to get. There was a pause for a second then he spoke.

"Come home baby, I miss you and my son." He pleaded sounding sincere

"I miss you too baby, but I can't it's not good for me nor you."

"I will change I promise, I just want my family back." He begged as baby Steve crawled his way up my legs to lay on my lap.

"Mommy, Mommy can I have a Krabby Patty like Sponge Bob for dinner tomorrow?" he asked sounding so happy. I had no choice but to chuckle.

"Yeah we can baby." I answered baby Steve's question but ignored his father's.

"Do you want to talk to your son?"

"Yeah, put him on the phone."

I handed the phone to baby Steve. "Hey, Daddy." His eyes lit up like the sky on July 4. "I miss you too daddy." Baby Steve continued. "Nothing, watching Sponge Bob with mommy." The more my son talked to his father the more my guard began to weaken. "I can't wait to see you too." Baby Steve turned and glanced at me. "Daddy said he loves you."

"Tell him I love him too."

Baby Steve handed me the phone "Daddy wants to talk to you."

"Okay. Thanks, baby." I said in my motherly voice.

"Shay baby, come back home please, I'll book a trip for the three of us to go to Hawaii." My guard broke like the levee in New Orleans back in 2005 and Steve was Hurricane Katrina. "Okay. I'll come home tomorrow."

"Oh for real?" His tone filled with excitement and I couldn't help but to be excited myself. We were going to be a family because it had to work.

…

After work, I was determined to go home to my man but for some reason he wasn't answering his phone. I called again, again, and again still no answer. Instantly my woman's intuition kicked in and planted a seed in my mind that Steve was at home with another woman. Instead of picking Baby Steve up from daycare early I decided to head straight to the house. I was speeding through traffic, dipping in and out of lanes on Penn Avenue determined to make a fifteen-minute trip to the North Side five minutes. The closer to home I got the more red lights stopped me in my tracks. My blood pressure was building to an all-time high, I was so eager to get to the house my fingers were shaking. I called once again and like the hundredth time no answer. Two blocks away from home at the intersection of East North Ave and Brighton Road a line of cars with orange flags trailing a black limousine and a black hearse crossed as soon as the light turned green for me to ride through.

"FUCK," I said slapping the steering wheel like it was the steering wheel's fault.

As soon as the lengthy line of funeral cars passed after watching two green lights alternate from yellow, red back to green my phone rang, rapidly my heart did cartwheels in my stomach.

"My man is calling me." I thought as I hurried to reached for the phone on the passenger's seat. On the caller ID, it read "Jay." Not who I expected. Jay is a nice guy with lot of potential, but I want my family back. I ignored the call then flew to the house going about 100 in a 25mph lane.

"Whoever this bitch is she's going die with Steve." I thought as I burned the tires when I made an instantaneous stop in front of the house. Swiftly I strolled out the car then did a slight jog through the front yard onto the porch with my keys in hand. I rapidly slid the key in the door then rushed into the house like the US Marshals. I scanned the living room there was no sign of him, I strolled straight to the bedroom and the he was lying in bed by with his boxer briefs on and socks sleeping with the box the engagement ring was in. The storm I once had calmed, I felt so foolish.

"Hey, baby." I said pushing Steve's shoulder gently to wake him up. He wiped his eyes adjusting them to the summer afternoon sunlight beaming from the window.

"Baby." He said in a sleepy groggy voice.

"Yes." I kissed him on the forehead.

"What you doing home so early?" He said with excitement as he sat up.

"They let me go early today."

"Oh, Okay." He said then continued. "Here put this on." He opened the box then slid the ring on my finger. "Can you give me one more chance to be your future husband?"

"Yes, Yes Steve." Tears filled up in my eyes then cascaded down my cheeks.

"I promise on my son I will never put my hands on you again." He reminded me glaring into my eyes then he slowly leaned in for a kiss.

"I miss you so much." He mentioned in between kisses.

"I miss you too." Gradually he pecked my cheek then went down to my neck planting soft passion kisses that caused me let out a soft moan. His kisses went from the neck down to the chest.

"I will never put my hands on you." He repeated as I laid back on the bed. I felt uncomfortable and insecure as he lowered his head down my body and lifted my scrub top up to kiss my stomach full of stretch marks. His tongue ran laps without hurrying around my belly button.

"This is mines." He muttered in the time he yanked my pants half way down my thighs.

"Yes, It's yours," was my response at the moment as he slithered his tongue at a slow pace tenderly across my pelvis. My pussy was wetter than an open fire hydrant in the hood on a hot day, my clit was throbbing so much it was screaming.

"EAT ME DADDY."

Steve removed my pants along with my underwear, tossed them to the floor, spread my legs away from each other, then glided his tongue up my left thigh to make a wet trail to the sweet spot. The fact that I was on a drought of no sexual intercourse for three weeks made me a time bomb ready to blow.

"Mmmh." I parted my lips to let out a soft moan.

He clamped his pussy eating soft lips around my clit and slid his wet tongue across as he sucked with compassion. Licking side to side generating friction against my love button.

"Oh my Gosh." I moaned "Yes!" I grasped the back of his head swaying my hips up and down, thrusting his mouth with my pussy.

"Yes, daddy, Yes." I motivated him.

"Keep going daddy, keep going." I was literally fucking his face.

"Ummm, Ummm, Ummm." He murmured like my lady fruit was his mother's best cooking on Sunday.

"I'm cumming, I'm cumming," I announced, pushing his head with more power.

My thrusts paused for a slight second then I let loose. "OH MY GOSH." my bones went from stiff to a rubber band as I came all over his chin.

For the next three to four hours, we made love until it was time to pick baby Steve up. We actually were a half an hour late getting him so we were expecting the $25 late fee charge on Friday.

One week Later

A week passed, and I was glad to say my family was together as one. Baby Steve was in his glory and to see my son's face light up with fireworks when he was with his father made my heart melt. Steve may have been a piece of shit boyfriend or fiancé in the past, but he was a phenomenal father, their father and son bond was stronger than a bridge that held cars and trucks. Even though Steve came home after midnight nearly every day; it didn't matter to me as long as he was home before the morning sunlight. I cherished every moment of the time we spent as family for the fact that there's nothing like having a happy home and most importantly raising our son together.

Jay and I texted occasionally mainly "good morning" messages and "How are you doing?" to keep tabs on each other. He was nothing more than a friend. Sure, he was very respectful, caring and not to mention very appealing to the eyes than Steve will ever be but I invested so much in my relationship and family, that starting all over with another man was not an option. When I broke the news to Jay that I was trying to make matters work with Steve, he was skeptical at first, but he supported my decision and understood the importance of family.

"If you ever need to talk, I'm always here to listen." He reminded me when I last visited him in the bank five days ago.

Today was Steve's 28th birthday. It was 10:20 am and I was at work busting my ass running around the busy chaotic hospital. I kind of regretted coming in that day.

"Instead of requesting to get off at 12:00 PM I should've just took the whole damn day off." I thought as I took a breath before stepping foot in room 311 on the third floor with my clipboard in one hand and a bottle of medicine in the other. Out of the twelve patients I was assigned to Ms. Davis. She was a skinny dark skin elderly lady in her mid-80's she complained to and cursed at anyone that came through the door. She rang the help button practically every five minutes.

"Finally, I get some fucking an assistance." She uttered in her deep voice, as she struggled to sit up in the hospital bed.

"Ms. Davis what's the problem now?" I calmly spoke ignoring her ignorance.

"You took so damn long I fucking forgot. Ugh…" She paused for a second "Oh yeah, can you put the news on for me?"

"The news? She called me in here to put the fucking news on. I just wanted to put her in a wheelchair and push her out this damn building." I thought as I serenely said, "Okay." I reached for the remote control that was sitting literally right next to her then flipped the channel to the KDKA News.

"Since I'm here, you mines 'well take your prescription."

"I don't want to take that shit." She said with an Mr. Yuck face.

"Ms. Davis the doctor recommends you take your prescription three times a day." In the time, I deliver the message to Ms. Davis what the doctor indicated my phone rang in my pocket.

"Fuck what the doctor says. He's not my father! My father died four years ago."

Quickly I grasp the phone out my pocket to peek at the name on the caller ID; It was Steve. I ignored the call then placed the phone back in my pocket then gave the devilish lady her drugs. When I escaped out of 311 I swiftly made my way into the employees only bathroom and locked the door then called my fiancé.

"Hello." He answered after the phone rang twice.

"Hey, birthday boy." I said in a playful sexy voice, he gave me a half giggle.

"Hey, baby. How's work?" "It's overwhelming today, I can't wait to get off and spend time with you for your birthday."

"Shit, I can't wait either babe. I'm about to leave the house right now I'm going to my mother's house for brunch then I have to run a few errands, I'll probably be home around four or four thirty." He stated.

"Good." I thought, I had errands to run as well, I ordered Steve his favorite strawberry cake specially made by Paddy Cake Bakery in Bloomfield on the east side and because I'm such a last-minute person I have to make a desperate stop past Robinson Mall to get his gifts. Rather than eating out at a fancy restaurant I needed to swing by the grocery store to pick up a few items for my famous lasagna that he absolutely loved. My intention was to put on a surprising show for him in my black see-through sexy lingerie lace bra set after the five-star candle light dinner and a warm bath with candles around and red roses floating on the water.

"Okay, baby have fun and tell your Ms. Johnson I said hi."

"What time you get off?" he asked.

"Umm at my usually time. Four o'clock." I spoke low and hesitancy.

"Hold on one second my mom on the other line." He uttered in the hurry.

"No babe, how about I talk to you later I have to get back to work."

"Okay, Love you babe."

"Love you too." I said the then phone call ended.

11:56 AM OFF WORK.

Going against the grain as employees, visitors and patients strolled towards the hospital entranced, I walked the opposite direction to make my way to the parking lot with my shades covering my eyes and phone glued to my ear on this sunny muggy day. The temperature had to be in the high 80's but the humidity made it feel like 150.

"What time will you be picking up your son tomorrow? I have a doctor's appointment at 10:00 PM." My mother asked in her grandmotherly voice. She was always a strong believer in spoiling the hell out her grandson, when he comes home he turns into a complete cry baby.

"I'll be there around eight before work, so I'll have time to pick him up and take him to daycare." I replied as I fished around in my purse for my keys.

"Okay, please let the daycare know I'm picking him up today."

"I will mom and thank you, I appreciate you so much." I retrieved the keys then pressed the unlock button.

"You're welcome Shay." Her tone changed to concern.

"I'll talk to you later mom." I opened the door then sat in the scorching hot car and instantaneously sweat beads formed on my forehead and cascaded down my beauty features. If the temperature felt like 150 degrees outside it surly felt like 200 in there.

"Talk to you later baby. Love you." It took me a second to return the love back for the fact that I was fiddling with the air conditioner and pressing down on the button to roll down the power windows as I struggled to inhale the little bit of new air coming through the windows.

"Love you too mom." I huffed.

"Shay." She said softly then paused. "Be careful."

"I will mom, I'll talk to you tomorrow."

Despite the fact she disapproved of me running back into the arms of the man that blacked my eye she still agreed to watch baby Steve for tonight for his birthday.

Normally when I get off work at five the rush hour traffic would move sluggishly like snails racing; for the reason that I was fortunate to escape hell early the traffic managed to move swiftly. I accomplished to get the groceries, explore the mall to shop and purchased the cake within two hours. I hurried through each store determined to get home before Steve; So, I could decorate the house with roses, candles, set the tables up like a five-star restaurant and prepare dinner. I grew anxious and irritated at the same time as traffic thickened on the way home. The cars were piling up like Tetris and for some odd reason I seemed to get every damn red light.

"Fuck!" I blurted in frustration as another red light changed right in front of my eyes, I was contemplating on running straight through the red like a tampon but there was a police vehicle posted on the right side of the road, probably recording speedy drivers. When the light flipped to green, I received a text.

"I just want you to know that I'm thinking about your pretty ass." Steve sent. Right away, my irritated frown turned into a smile. I drove a half of mile to distance myself from police before texting back.

"I'm stinking about you too" I texted while driving. Seconds after sending him the text I realized my typo, so I corrected my error. "Thinking about lol."

"Lol oh your stinking about me." He replied.

"I guess lmbo"

"Love you, I just wanted you to know that." He texted with a kissy face emoji. Traffic was moving a little faster.

"Thank You God." I thought as I press weighty on the gas.

"Love you too babe."

2:39 PM I finally arrived home and there were 15 to 20 bags in the trunk that I was responsible to lug alone into the apartment. This was a time I sure wished Steve was present to assist me with carrying these bags. To avoid making three journeys back and forth I carried six bags in each hand, I struggled to Hulk them through the front yard onto the porch. When I lowered the bags down to the Pittsburgh Steelers door mat to make a second trip I spotted Steve's car parked across the street. The first thought that came to mind was he was riding his motorcycle today. I grabbed the remainder of the bags in one hand and carried the cake in the other then closed the trunk with my elbow. Somehow, I managed to slide the key in the door awkwardly as I held the groceries and cake in hand. I pushed the door gently with my knees, the door slowly swung open. When I stepped foot in the apartment I caught sight of an unfamiliar Louie hand bag. Right away a smile spread across my face then erased rapidly when I heard moaning.

"Prince baby, fuck me harder daddy, harder." between a squeaking bed. The color of my skin faded, my fingers trembled with devastation and my heartbeat raced while a bitch screamed Steve's nickname in pleasure.

"Prince, oh my gosh prince!" She wailed so loud I was certain the neighbors could hear.

The world appeared to move in slow motion as I stood in the doorway in disbelieve.

"This can't be real; this can't be happening." I thought hoping I was dreaming.

"This is my fucking pussy." Steve declared as the bed squeaked consistently.

After I came to the conclusion this wasn't a fucking nightmare I dropped the bags to the floor and didn't bother to shut the front door. I placed the cake on the coffee table. With quivering legs, I slowly strolled towards the bedroom where the door was cracked enough for me to see an eye burning sight of a light skin woman riding Steve's dick, sliding up and down while her ponytail bounced up in down at the same rhythm as now my ex fiancé laid helplessly on his back on top of our mattress with his feet planted to the floor while thrusting up inside her. I was going to make a dash to the kitchen to grab a knife to stab the bitch in the back then cut Steve cheating ass dick off but I have a son that needed me so that thought vanished as baby Steve came to mind. Each step I took felt like I was walking on fire stones, the sex noises increased louder and louder, he slapped her ass hard putting a red hand print on her butt. I stood in the doorway for two seconds then I blacked out storming into the bedroom with rage. I pulled her whole body off his dick from the ponytail like pulling carrots out of dirt. She flopped to the floor in fear

"Oh My God Shay." She screamed with her hands up covering her face while I throw hard connecting punches at my former friend hoe ass Alisha's face. Between each and every punch I blurted curse words out with anger.

"You sneaky." *Punch* "Ass." *Punch*. In the time, I hit Alisha I heard Steve scream.

"Oh shit, oh shit what the fuck." His heart probably was about to fall out his chest.

"Bitch." Punch "I should kill you." I huffed and puffed blowing steam as I gave her a combination of punches. When I finished smashing her bloody face with my fist I stood up then kicked her in the stomach at the same time I uttered "BITCH!"

I glared at her worthless body on the floor like a piece of shit as I shivered with terror and misery then I disrespectfully spit in her face. "BITCH GET THE FUCK OUT MY HOUSE, FOR I KICK YOUR ASS SOME MORE!" I said retrieving the booty shorts and white shirt off the floor, throwing at her. "GET THE FUCK OUT!" I demand through gritted teeth.

I shot my eyes at Steve standing in the corner of the room next to the nightstand speechless with regret; his eyes were wider than two half of dollar coins.

"I guess this is the bitch A in your phone huh?" I chuckled. All men know when a woman laughs, smiles, or chuckles in a sticky situation that means don't fuck with her. She liable to act like a bitch from hell. I was sure Steve sensed the homicide in my eyes, no word would slip out his mouth all I received was an anxious grin as Alisha made an effort to peel herself off the floor.

"Huh, is that what you want Steve?" My tone got louder as I pushed Alisha to the bed as she tried to slide her pants on. He just scratched his head then sat on the right side of the bed.

"No, No I want you babe." He pleaded with a bullshit answer. The bitch got fully dressed then darted out the room. All I heard was the screen door slam.

"Why? Steve Why?" I questioned him, I was so fucking hurt tears refused to fall from my eyes. He didn't have an answer he was back to speechless.

"You know what I'm done, I deserve better. You can run around and fuck these hoes without me in your life. I can do better by myself." I said then peacefully walked out the bedroom door.

"Babe," I heard a slight squeak in the bed. "Wait babe I'm sorry." He was on my tail as I grabbed the keys on the table. Now he was a foot away standing right in front of me with tears streaming down his face.

"I fucked up. I really fucked up." He pleaded with his hands on his temples.

"Sorry, I'm done." I pulled the lid off the cake then swiftly smashed the shit in his face.

"Happy Birthday Bitch." I uttered then strolled out the front door leaving all my problems in the house. Luckily, he didn't chase me down to put his hands on me, instead he just stood there knowing he fucked up. Now it was time to call a friend.

JAY
Two Years Later

I kneeled to my knees in front of family and friends at my family reunion on this beautiful July day. Life was considerable, many blessing poured on me since I modified my way of living. Other than get promoted to branch manager at the Oakland branch my relationship was healthy and I could honestly say I have a spectacular woman. Once the boy she once called her man threw her to the gravel like a dusty rock, it took a man like me to notice a diamond surrounded by pebbles. I picked the diamond up and cherished the ground she walked on with stability, respect and unconditional love.

Two years ago, this exact day July 23 at 11:11 PM in the middle of typing my apartment address to this shorty Layla I had met a couple days earlier a phone call interrupted as I relaxed on the duct taped up couch covering up the space where Amber slashed. I sent the text then answered the phone in a hurry. I was sure this person wanted to chat about her man but I was her good friend.

"Hello." I said with excitement

"Hey, Jay are you busy?" The woman on the other end uttered sounding slightly ruined.

"Um, um, just sitting on the couch watching TV on my cracked screen." I snickered.

"Where you live? I want to see you." Her tone was desperate. That shit caught me completely off guard.

"You want to see me? Right now," I paused for a second then gazed at the red diagonal numbers on the cable box "You want to come over at 11:13?"

"You know what I think this is a bad idea I'm sorry." She quickly changed her mind.

"No, No, no it's just was unexpected, I thought you would be with your man since it's his born day." I said with confusion in my voice.

"What's your address I'm coming over?"
I sent the woman of my dreams the address and came up with a convincing lie to deter Layla from coming over, she was skeptical at first but she rerouted and went elsewhere after I beat whatever bullshit fib I blubbered in her head. Within 20 minutes, I buzzed the woman in the apartment building. Less than five minutes later she knocked on my door. Although I knew who was standing in the doorway by habit I glared through the peek hole, I smile as my one eye caught sight of her breath-taking beauty. Without

hurrying I swung the door open and was puzzled when I saw she was dressed in a trench coat in the middle of summer. The central air blanketed the apartment with a slight chill and the only light that beamed in the place was coming from the television.

"You, you look flawless." I eyeballed her stunning freckles on her gorgeous face and admired the designer heels she was wearing.

"Thank you." We embraced tightly for a good minute.

"Damn I missed you." I kissed her warm left cheek.
"I missed you too." She spoke softly, her expression showed misery. As an alternative of sorrow, I decided to reverse the mood of the sudden doleful environment that crept in my apartment through laughter. When we let go of each other's embrace, in a joking matter I said

"Welcome to Jay's apartment." Sounding joyful, spreading my arms wide as if I lived in a luxury mansion. I pointed to the couch with the duct tape covering the slashes.

"Right here we have the famous wounded couch with tape covering up the cuts." If the TV wasn't on, I swear to God you would've been able to hear a feather drop, not even a smile curved on her pretty face. She just stood there in the center of the living room floor with her coat on like a Statue of Liberty gazing at me.

"Are you okay?" I cut short the corny jokes, slowly sat down on the couch, and glanced at her with concern.

"Yes, I'm Okay. But this is the reason why I'm here." She pulled the belt to her coat loose; the fabric slid slowly off her shoulder then hit the floor. Soon as I got a glimpse of what was under the coat I was displeased, disappointed, upset, and ashamed all in one. The fat remarks she said her ex-boyfriend uttered played in my head repeatedly.

"You fat bitch."

"Ever since you had the baby you got fat."

At that moment, I had very little to say, I just hoped the words that were on the tip of my tongue didn't hurt her pride. I took a deep breath before speaking a single word as I stared a hole through her probably with a face of unsatisfactory. She seemed worried and stood their looking like she made the biggest mistake in her life.

"What?" she said looking bewildered.

"Look," I paused. "I understand you came here with intentions on having an amazing night. You're one attractive woman that I can see myself being with and growing old with but I am not your ex-boyfriend. I'm not going judge you no type of way." She stood in the same spot with ears glued to my every word as I continued, "So before we do anything I want you to take that fucking t-shirt off right now. I don't give a fuck about a little bit of stretch marks." Her eyebrows raised. I suppose she was surprised and speechless at the same time. She hesitantly removed the t-shirt from over her body to reveal a black see through lingerie matching bra and thong set. My jaw fell straight to the floor as my eyeballs bubbled with hearts. She was drop dead gorgeous, in no time my man hood fully grew inside my basketball shorts causing me to make a tent in the private area.

"Come here," I demanded. She kicked the heels off, swayed her way towards me with more confidence in her step then stood right between my legs as I scooted to the edge of the couch. She glared down into my eyes showing no emotion on her features, I reached around her waist and pulled her closer as I firmly grabbed hold of both of her butter soft booty cheeks. Her plain face expression turn into a slight grin; I shot a grin back, exposing my left dimple while biting my bottom lip. I planted my lips on her stomach and made an effort to kiss on every last delightful tiger stripe she earned.

I worked my lips passionately down the pelvis leaving a wet trail. I worked my lips passionately down to the pelvis leaving a wet trail, she sighed as pleasure escaped her lips as I continued to head down to the gold mine. I glared up, she was looking down at me like an angel from heaven with her eyes nearly open as she watched me perform. I let go of her one of her cheeks and with the free hand, I gently slid the thin material to the side. With my thumb, I spread one side of her pussy lips apart to expose the pleasure button; I filled my mouth with saliva then gently clamp my lips around her clit. I slide my tongue back and forth, she let out a soft moan as I felt her quiver as if her knees began to become weak. Not even a minute I swung her down to the damaged couch, drop to my knees, removed the thong and spread her legs apart to devour the fruit I've had a desire to eat since day one. I was eating that pussy like a homeless man with a steak in front of him

"Oh my gosh yes, yes" she wailed as my tongue slid back and forth like a paint brush.

"I'm cumming, I'm cumming" the woman announced as I sucked, licked, and munched the fuck out of her pussy while breathing heavily out of my nose. I was determined to make this woman cum so hard she would shrink. Constantly I flapped my tongue around the clit non-stop as my saliva and her juices flowed down my chin and on to the couch. The closer to an orgasm the heavier she pressed down on my head and the louder she moaned with gratification.

"Oh my Gosh. Oh, my Gosh!" her back launched about ten inches off the couch, taking her to the fucking moon. She let out a blaring scream in the time her back lands in the same spot of the couch where it launched. She placd her hands over the face while attempting to catch her breath.

"Oh my." In between words, she huffed. "God this" inhale "was the" exhale "I ever" inhale "had." exhale, her chest heaving in and out.
Before she could fully catch her breath, she signaled for me to come up for a kiss. I crawled over top her body and leaned in for an innocent kiss with her pheromones fragrance coating mouthpiece. The

innocent pecks escalated to our tongues getting tangled like headphone cords, her kisses were sweet as our first kiss but with a lot more passion. Suddenly I felt her hand creeping up my shorts and clamping onto my hard manhood.

"I want this." She said in a sexy tone as soon as we untied our tongues. In seconds, she flopped my wood out the shorts and massaged precisely at a slow pace while glaring into my pleasurable squint eyes. Each stroke felt electrifying she had hands of a professional I can just imagine how pleasing the head game can be.

Unfortunately, head wasn't on the playlist for tonight and that was okay with me my goal was to be the pleaser. We resumed kissing again tonguing one other down like there's no tomorrow on the schedule. In the time, we kiss she gradually slid my shorts halfway down my thighs; I gave her a hand and push the shorts down to my feet then step over to fully remove from my body.

I lift her legs up over my shoulders then gradually plug ever inch inside bit by bit. The inside of her **** gave me a toe curling sensation, chills bulge on the surface of my brown skin. I felt as if I have sunk in a pleasuring pone of quicksand, she was unbelievable wet. A man with a weak mind with no sexual control will fold under pressure for sure. She gasps for air "Oh my Gosh it's so big." She let out a moan that boosted my ego. I dug in and out slowly in a missionary position within five minutes we were fucking like zoo animals. We went hard and had to

82

switch potions at least six times. Sweaty, hot rough sex, by her body motion I noticed she liked to be choked. She loved when I pulled her hair. Or me to pull her hair and the shit that caught me off guard was that she requested for me to slap her in the face. We must've fucked for hours on the couch and even went to sleep on it. After that spectacular night, she was officially my woman. She was literally my soulmate that God delivered to me himself, not only was the sex remarkable but she was amazing in all departments. She kept good conversations, was supportive, she put her two cents in on every goal and idea I have to paint a better picture. We even talked about our problems instead of lashing out at each other. There was trust, love and respect between the both of us. For the reason for this woman to be so phenomenal is the reason why I'm on my knees in front of my family and the guest family that I love. I pulled the ring out my pocket and smiled at her shocked yet nervous expression. "Shaylin will you marry me?"

With excitement written all over, her beautiful face and tears flowing down her cheeks she gave me the best answer a person ever utter.

"Yes, Jay Yes." Cheers from family and friends erupted with happiness.

Another man's trash is another man's treasure.

Message from the author Tinker Jeffries

First and for most I want to take a moment to thank everyone who read this story "Can't Dispose Gold." I also would like to thank my editor Chardaè for making time edit in between her busy schedule. Honestly, this was supposed to be at least five pages but turn out to my 50 pages.

I wrote this piece to wake up the people who are stuck in the identical situation. There people who are miserable in their relationship but mange to stay because their scared to be alone, accustomed to the cycle of living, afraid of a new begin, addicted to an unhealthy love, sex, and luxury things the man or woman offers. For one love has no price, love shouldn't be force because of child or environment that you are used to. Before love there should be a friendship and most important RESPECT AND TRUST without those three there's no deep love. You can love someone to death but may not be in love with them. There's a whole another world than being miserable, depressed, and unwanted. Somebody else will love all your flaws and all your goods and treat you like the King and Queen God made you to be.

002. CLEAN LAUNDRY

WEEK ONE

I lugged a heavy bag full of dirty clothes and a bottle of Tide Laundry Detergent as I made my way through the hallways and down the elevator to the basement floor. 3 AM on a Thursday night was always the best time for me to wash clothes. Most of the residents were in bed not thinking about laundry and I had the entire room to myself. At 3am I never had to worry about anyone hogging machines or leaving their clothes in them. Washing four loads at the same time was my usual and I got shit done within an hour if I was on my shit.

It ain't nothin' cut that bitch off, I nodded as music played through my headphones. *So what you sayin' hoe, you know I'm the man hoe,* I placed four quarters in two washers, poured the detergent into the machines, and let the hot water fill halfway before dumping my clothes inside. I stopped at the vending machine to feed my sweet tooth feeling like I earned the right to do so. I grabbed a Twizzler, a bag of BBQ Chips, and moved on to the next machine to grab an Orange pop to wash the chips down. I stuck my hand through the bottom opening to grab my pop and froze as I caught a reflection on the glass. Someone was dragging a basket of clothes through the door and I instantly grew irritated as the door flung open.

"Oh! You scared me. I didn't know anyone was in here sorry. "

I turned around and pulled my earphones out my ears pretending I didn't hear her. "What you say?"

"Nothing I wasn't expecting any one to be in here." She smiled staring me down.

The woman was breathtaking as she stood there in her Victoria Secret Pink Shorts stopping high up showing her golden-brown legs and thick thighs. She smiled showcasing her perfect teeth along with a stunning smile and beautiful lips. Like a gun to the temple, she blew my mind. I kept my composure like I wasn't interested, because I didn't want her to feel like I was a thirsty animal.

"My bad didn't mean to scare you. You okay?"

"Yes." I softened up a bit speaking with sincerity. "Okay, do you need help carrying that basket, you look like you struggling." I took a few steps towards her to help but she refused.

"No, it's okay I got it, but thank you." Her smiled never left her mouth as she continued to struggle with her basket.

"You're welcome love." I plugged my earphones back in the sat down as I scrolled through Instagram and ate my snacks. It was challenging to pay attention to the pictures on the screen of my phone. I was tied up peeking at her phat ass while she was bending over to grab clothes out the basket.

The moment was awkward when she finished loading the machine, she sat on the opposite side from me with her legs crossed on the table. We both were silently for a few minutes as our thumbs swiped across our phone screens. I sat and listened to my music as the scent of detergent filled the room with the familiar scent of fresh flowers in the summer time. I felt her get a glimpse of me, but she didn't say a word. *"Should I say something? Should I break this awkward silence?"*

I glanced at her catching her staring me down this time. I smiled letting her know she was busted. Quickly she dropped her eyes and gained focus to her phone. *"Fuck it I'm going to speak,"* I thought to myself. I pulled my earphones out and thought of a million things I could say to her. Before any of my thoughts could escape my lips, her phone rang. She stood up from the chair and smiled at me as she made her way out the door.

"Hey babe are you here?" She spoke answering the phone.

I sucked my teeth feeling like a failure for missing an opportunity to approach this woman with beautiful features. I put the clothes in the dryer and set the time for thirty minutes and as soon as I sat in the chair, she opened the door and stepped in with this tall light skin nigga who had a beard and a short haircut.

"Did you watch my stuff?" She questioned walking past with a bright smile.

I slightly laughed, "Nah not really, nobody came in here through."

"That's the reason why I wash clothes late."

"Me too, I wouldn't even attempt to come in here during the day."

"I just moved here two months ago, I came down here to wash clothes around five after work; all the machines were taken then some lady told me a guy used three washers and left his clothes in there for hours"

"Aww I hate that shit, I'm not touching nobody's clothes even if they were washed a thousand times."

I glanced over at dude standing quietly next to the

vending machine; he nodded his head "What's up?

I nodded. "What's up?" I responded back.

"How do you like living here in the East Side Hightower?" I stopped her before she could take a few steps to leave.

"So far, I love it, everyone's so respectful and quiet. It's a big step from Robinson Projects, that's what I know."

"Damn, you're from Robinson? Them niggas is crazy as fuck over in uptown."

She shrugged her shoulders twisting her lips. "I know, don't judge me."

"Nah, I'm not judging you, you can be from the hood and still be classy. But I'm not trying to hold y'all up, my name is Vick I live on the fourth floor. What's yours?"

"Chell..."

I glanced over at her man. "Yo, what's your name bra?"

"Tayon"

"Oh okay, that's your girl?"

"Something like that." Tayon gave short answers and was obviously too cool for conversation but I shrugged it off.

"Aww man you're a lucky dude dawg, keep her she's a pretty woman."

His facial expression turned red when I complimented the beauty of his girl. She smiled appreciating the compliment and he noticed immediately.

"I know!! Good look, alright yo we're about to go upstairs homie I'm tired."

WEEK TWO

2:40 am

"Oh What's up luv? You late night wash again." I smiled spotting her again in the laundry room.

"Yea I'm back in here." Chell sighed staring at the basket of clothes. "I have clothes for days that I need to wash; I figured I'll do little by little each day."

I opened the washer top. "Whatever you got to do I know that feeling."

"You use hot water for your colors?" She walked over and leaned on the washer machine next to mine.

"Yeah, why?"

She smiled and quickly turned the knob to cold. Use cold water, unless you want your colored shirts to fade, use hot only for whites."

I laughed appreciating the advice. "Look at you trying to teach me how to wash clothes. I've been on my own since 18 and I never knew that."

"Most men are clueless when it comes down to house chores."

I threw the clothes in the machine amused with her statement." Do your man help with the shit around the house?"

"I don't have a man that dude you seen me with the other day is my ex. I only use him for dick but if I had a man I'd rather for him to chill and let me handle the cooking and cleaning."

"Shit majority of the females don't think like that now days, you can't even get a bowl of cereal from these lazy ass chicks. But I do like to do some things, I don't mind taking the trash out or washing dishes."

"That's good, you can take my trash out for me then." Her smile brightened as she stared me down.

"Well let me know I'll take it out just because you're attractive."

"You're cute yourself so where's your lady?"

I took a few steps and sat down in the chair pretending to need to think about the answer. "I'm single, I talk to a couple females; nothing serious though."

"Uhh, you know when a guy says, *"nothing serious"* that means he's fucking with someone heavy."

"I'm dead ass serious! I don't fuck with anybody like I said I fuck around with a few ladies." There was no hint of playfulness in my tone.

"Whatever nigga." She rolled her eyes in disbelief taking a seat next to me.

"What you mean whatever, shit your fucking with your old man I guess there's feelings still there."

"No, I wouldn't dare put myself in that situation again, that nigga can talk to whoever he wants, I'm not the jealous type of person, I been over him. He just knows how to fuck me the way I love to fuck." she spoke candidly as if I knew her for more than a week.

"You must've tried something new and the sex wasn't good huh?"

"Oh God, I wasted my time with this guy I was really into, he was respectable, good looking, he had his shit together, but the SEX was not pleasing. He bragged and bragged; like he was going to beat the pussy up, come to find out he didn't know what the hell he was doing."

"Damn!" I smirked

"I was soo irritated and turned off after we did it."

"What you do? Stop talking to him because the sex was wack?" I was now invested in this story beyond curious.

"Yes, I couldn't move on with him. I like to be fucked, pull my hair, choke me up, smack my ass I like for a man to be aggressive and know how to throw the dick. That's the reason why I go back to my ex from time to time"

I scratched my forehead and bit my bottom lip getting a little turned on by her words. My mind was racing with thoughts of my body between her legs knocking down all her walls. "So you like your hair pulled, you like to get choked up and you like a nigga to smack that ass? Okkkkky you must be a little freak!"

She shrugged her shoulders. "I might be, every woman has a little bit of freak in them, the right guy has to bring it out."

I smiled like a pervert no longer ashamed of my curiosity. "Humm is that right?" Sexual thoughts ran through my mind like a horse race.

She grinned reading my mind. "Boy you better stop," she warned knowing I was thinking about her.

"What!!! I didn't say anything." I smirked staring her down.

"Okay let's get off this conversation before you think with that little head of yours." She laughed pointing to my crotch.

WEEK THREE

Sitting on the edge of the couch in my dark living room with the television on, my legs were stiff as I got head from some chick I met at a local bar a few weeks ago. She was on her knees between my thighs with her hands tightly wrapped on my dick. She twisted her wrist and putting in work while her mouth went down and up at the same pace. Her hands were sticky and drenched in saliva as I gripped a handful of her hair and put it in a ponytail. "Mmh Mmh suck that shit just like that, mmmh like that Mmh," I groaned watching her throw the neck. Noises of her slurping made the head feel ten times better as her head bobbed at a steady pace. She lifted her head up than licked the tip as she beat my dick to try to release the nut out. She saw it as a challenge staring at me and moaning determined to make me cum. I stared in her brown eyes and dug my toes deeper into the carpet. "Mmmmm keep going, keep going."

I felt the muscles contract as she sucked and beat constantly. The nut was creeping up towards the tip of my dick, ready to bust like she lit a wick on a stick of dynamite. Up and down her head went and I was bracing myself as chills ran through my body.

"Oh shit oh shit" I said as I attempted to remove my dick from her mouth before I bust.

"Unn umm" she pushed my hand away and kept going surprising the shit out of me.

She moaned as she continued sucking and sucking; saliva dripping everywhere, my dick was slippery wet.

"Oh shit, oh shit, Oh shit!" I said as I felt my bones tighten.

"Ummmmm," cum flew out my dick and squirted all inside her mouth; shooting to the back of her throat. Her eyes were watery, hand was full of saliva and cum. She slowed the pace and glanced in my eyes before squeezing my dick tight like a freeze pop to get every last drop.

When she finished I pulled my boxer briefs up and tucked my dick inside. "Do you want a rag or something for your hands?" I was polite.

She nodded her head "Yes, please."

I jumped off the couch then made my way in the bathroom, I handed her the warm wet rag and sat on the couch watching as she pulled herself together.

"Too bad you're on your period, I love me a chocolate woman I would've tore that pussy up, and you're thick too."

She laughed. "Maybe next time, but you're delicious I can suck that anytime."

"Is that right, we'll I'll have you on speed dial, you made me bust fast as fuck you know what you doing." I sat with a grin on my face.

When she got settled, she sat on the couch and grabbed the remote control. "Can I see what's on the Lifetime Channel?"

"Yeah, go head babe, do you want something to drink" Were the only words I could utter while my brain was in overdrive thinking of a plan to get her out my apartment

"Water with ice, thank you."

I stood up and grabbed my iPhone off the table then went into the kitchen, I texted my homie Leon.

Leon: Famo what's the deal?

Me: Yo I need you to call my phone in five minutes say your car broke down on the parkway, I'm trying to get this chick out my house.

Leon: alright I got you, did you hit tho?

Me: Nah I just got the neck, but do that for me.

Leon: Bet, five minutes…

I grabbed us both a bottle of cold spring water and sat on the couch next to her. I even wrapped my arm around her body pretending like I wanted this to go on all night.

"What you watching?"

"This movie about a wife killing her husband because she's feed up with the abuse, I watched half but I never caught the ending."

I snuck a glance at the time realizing five minutes passed two minutes ago and there was still no word from Leon. I was getting worried as I got sucked into the movie but a few seconds later the phone range and I picked it up on the second ring already knowing it was Leon. "Yo what's good?" I put Leon on speakerphone to sweeten the lie.

"Man, you have a gas can in your ride bra?" He said with disappointment.

"Why? You ran out of gas fam?"

"Yeah, I'm on the parkway on 279 going toward downtown I need you to slide through one time for me yo."

Portia glance at me with an upset face

"I'm over here cuddling with my boo but I got you, I'm bout to dip now."

"Good look, hit me when your close."

As soon as we hung up I jumped off the couch. "Damn babe I got to go help my nigga out, when the next time you'll be free?" I put on the most believable disappointed face as she followed me to the door and into the hallway towards the elevators.

"I get off at 5 everyday any time after and I'm free all day on the weekends, it's up to you."

"Swear, you got some of the best head I ever had" That was not a lie. I smiled as the elevator doors opened and I stood beside Portia. As we walked off, I glanced to the right and noticed Chell at the mailboxes standing with mail in her hand. She smiled while we strolled past and I just waved and said what's up. Low key I was excited deep down inside that she saw me with another woman. I wanted her to feel some type of way. I kind of hoped it would make her jealous to see if she was really into me or just fuckin' with me those days in the laundry room.

After escorting Portia to her vehicle, I made my way back to the apartment building. The short young black security guard stopped me before I could even make it to the elevator. "Man, I think shorty with the red hair digging you. She watched y'all two the whole way to the car. When you was coming back, she ran up the stairs."

I chuckled amused by her behavior but not completely surprised. "Oh yeah, ha ha that's funny as hell, did she look mad?" I wanted all the details.

"She was kinda upset."

I smiled as I wave my hand pass the elevator door to prevent it from closing

"Word, oh yeah she was upset, ha ha ol girl bad as fuck."

"Which one? The one you walked outside or the red head girl?"

"The chick with the red hair."

"No doubt she fine but I was loving the girl you was with."

"Word up, but look yo I have to go I'll see you round." I waved bye and headed back toward the elevator but stopped and turned around before getting in. "Ah, don't say nothing about what just happened because she'll know I said something."

"I won't, alright yo."

…

2:30 AM seemed like the perfect time to wash my white clothes and uniforms for work. I was all showered, ate, and comfy in a pair of hoop shorts, a V-Neck, and slippers. I couldn't wait to finish just to get into bed and crash. Standing in the elevator on my way to the laundry room it stopped before getting to the basement. I smiled staring at the number two and then a red haired Chell standing there with a rolling buggy, two baskets full of clothes and black garbage bag.

"Oh hey," she was the first to speak.

I chuckled as the elevator doors closed. "What's up? I swear you're a stalker. It's like you know when to wash clothes." I teased, and she rolled her eyes.

"I just like to wash late I don't stalk anyone, if anybody was doing the stalking that would be you."

I turned my face. "Oh, okay, how was your day?"

"Good," she gave a one-word answer.

"Well that's good, you're going to be down here all-night washing clothes." I tried to lighten the moment as the elevator opened on the ground floor and the two of us stepped out.

The elevator opened on the ground floor as we stepped out I said.

"I know."

"What's wrong? You seem down?" I didn't beat around the bush noticing in her voice and her demeanor that she was upset about earlier. She was all in her feelings and she wasn't even my girl.

"Nothing I'm fine." I didn't even know her well enough but I knew that was a lie. What woman is really fine when she tells you that she's fine?

"Nah something wrong, you're not talkative and outgoing today." I pushed.

"I'm fine, seriously."

I held the door as she rolled the buggy through.

"Okay, well I hope your night gets better."

I dropped the bag on top of washing machine next to the one I was using; I emptied the clothes into the machine while she struggled to lift the baskets out of the buggy.

"Do You need help?" I offer.

"No, I got it!!" She said with aggression.

I smiled kind of enjoying her attitude.

"Dang I'm just asking, you don't got to get smart"

Despite what she told me I closed the machine then approached her to help lift the second basket onto the washer; She poked her lips out and surprisingly didn't bite my head off for not listening. "Thank you, even though I don't like you."

"Why? There shouldn't be a reason not to like me I didn't do anything wrong."

"I know, I'm sorry, that's the problem I think DO like you, when I seen you with that little chick I got bothered, she was a little cutie though, I'll give her that." She scowled pouring the laundry detergent in as the water filled up.

I leaned against the washer beside the one she was using while she loaded the clothes inside.

"She is cute but that ain't about nothing and the crazy thing is, I feel the same way about you. Every time I'm down here I hope you bust through the door and come rape me."

"Come rape you?" She repeated what I said with a smile on her face and surprise in her tone.

"I didn't mean to say that." I crossed my arms across my chest knowing it was too late to take it back.

"Yes, you did."

"Yeah, I did; there's some things I want to do to you." It was finally in the air and I didn't want to take that back.

"Like what?" She spoke raising her eyebrows and giving me her full attention.

I slowly stepped behind her wrapped my arms around her body and kissed the back of her neck. "I can show you better than I can tell you."

She stepped to the side pushing me off of her and stared me down like she was thinking it over. "You must want my pussy."

"Nah That's not all I want but I ain't going to lie I would fuck the shit out of you."

She closed the washer and glanced my way rolling her eyes

"Oh my God you're straight forward."

"Sike nah, come here." I smiled grabbing her hand

bringing her towards me and my smile widened as she wrapped her arms around my lower waist.

"What? I got to put this other load in" she spoke trying to avoid the inevitable.

I looked down and then kissed her forehead. I lifted her chin up with my index finger to catch eye contact with her. "Mmm I want those lips," I said gently biting my bottom lip.

Softly our lips touched together, her lips were moist & smooth, after a few pecks our tongues tangled like computer cords as we leaned against the washing machine. I kissed the side of her neck then made my way down to the collarbone.

"Mmmmmmm…" she moaned.

I got a firm grip of her ass then our tongues tied again, she bit my bottom lip hard as fuck as she pushed away from my body.

"Why are you caressing me? What if someone walks in?"

"Ain't nobody coming in here everyone sleep… matter fact I'm going to put your basket against the door."

As soon as I grabbed the basket off the washer, she interrupted my plan. "That's not going to work, you need something better to hold the door, use that chair and put it under the door knob.

When she put her two cents in on blocking the door, I knew there was a chance I was fucking.

"Alright" I responded to her idea as she jumped up on the washer and sat down. I grabbed the only table chair in the laundry room and placed the chair under the knob and sat the basket on top. I stood between her legs as they dangled off the machine and pushed her upper body backwards. Quickly I lifted up her stomach and I licked around her belly button then I ran my tongue down to her pelvis. I yanked on her shorts as my lips went below the waist, lower and lower my tongue went the further I pulled her shorts down. When I removed her shorts I spread her legs open over my shoulders, slightly I bit her inner thighs then ran my tongue up toward her pussy. I licked between the labia with my wet tongue then ran it up the other thigh to tease her some more. She gently put her left hand behind my head as I reversed my tongue back up her thigh to put my face right in, I wrapped my lips around her soft clit then let my tongue slide back and forth like it was zip lining.

In the same time I'm licking, I'm sucking the pussy with a watery mouth; I could hear her breathing heavily and moaning to the pace of my tongue moving. I grabbed hold of both thighs and pushed her knees towards her chin for a better view of the pussy, I shook my face in between while my lips and tongue constantly remained massaging the same spot. Her grip tightened on the back of my skull. "I'm cummin oh myyyyy I'm cumin!"

I kept on licking until I chased the soul out of this woman's body, the orgasms forced her to straighten her legs as they shook, she pushed my forehead caught off guard.

"Pleeeseeee stop stop mmmmm" she begged moaning.

I pushed her hand away then put my face back in the pussy and continued to suck and lick her clit with a soft touch for a few seconds while I glance at her pretty face as she recuperated. She looked drained, but she didn't know that this was just the beginning. *I'm 'bout to work her body.*

"Damn I can't believe we just did that," she said with her sweet sexy voice as she smiled, she made her way down off the washer.

"Can't believe what?"

"Can't believe we're doing this in the laundry room."

"I know Unexpected sex is the best."

"Mmm mmh, well it's my turn, take your shirt off, and

give it to me."

I was clueless for why she needed my shirt, but I removed it ASAP like Rocky, then I handed the shirt over. She removed her shirt as well, all she had on was her bra and slippers. She balled both shirts up then dropped them to the floor; right when I attempted to speak she dropped to her knees.

"What you...oh you using those for knee pads?"

She didn't bother answering my question. She pulled the strings of my shorts and in no time my dick grew hard, long and strong; you would've thought I was toting a gun inside my shorts. Chell unhurriedly pulled my shorts down, my dick jumped out like a spring closed in a box. Immediately she grabbed hold of my manhood then spit on it to make it slippery, she licked the head as the washer cycle came to a halt but that didn't stop her. She spit on it once again for further lubrication, then she wrapped both hands around my penis and beat it with a twist in the wrists as she sucked all in the same time. Her head went back and forward, sucking and beating. She released the right hand then beat the dick fast and firm, the sound was wet and squishy, I felt chills run through my body as if I had just taken the ice water bucket challenge. She wrapped her mouth around the dick and threw her face at it, saliva dropped to the floor. She moaned and fingered herself with her free hand and I slid my hand through her red hair and palmed her scalp as I leaned against the washing machine.

Not even five minutes later, the nut rushed up my dick.

"Yo I'm bout to nut!"

She stopped sucking but continued to beat

"Don't cum in my mouth," her sweet voice turned stern before she went back to work sucking and beating. In seconds my knees got weak, I pushed her head back as the cum shot out.

"Ummmm damn yo!"

She kept on beating, I was losing my mind, the shit felt so fucking good that I was at a loss for words. She glanced at me with smiles then she stood to her feet.

My dick was still standing long and hard. I stood behind her to position myself; the sight of the back shot was appealing. She has a rose vine tattoo starting from her ass going up the rib cage along with the curly red hair and plum brown ass had me in lust. I bended her over against the washer, grabbed hold of her shoulder as I pressed down on the back to put an arch in her spine with the other hand, I plugged my dick inside her and gently pushed every inch I had to offer deep up in the tight wet pussy,

"Mmmm that dick is big mmmm damn baby mmmm!"

I pulled her body towards my body by the shoulder then I stroked at a steady mild pace in and out, in and out I was so deep in her water like a submarine that her ass jiggled as my dick went in.

"Mmm Mmm mmm mmm ow ow ow fuck!" She moaned with her hands spread over the washer. I bit my bottom lip at the feeling of her pussy suffocating my dick. Her moans were extremely too loud, to prevent us from getting snagged so I got a fist full of her hair then pulled it back while I covered her mouth with the other hand. I was beating the pussy up, stroking her insides giving her every inch, and all my energy.

There were three seats nailed in the floor. I grabbed the shirt she used as kneepads to cover the middle chair to protect my ass and she sat down on me facing the same direction and all I saw was her back and her red hair. She held my dick up then slid down slowly. In no time, she sped up bouncing her pussy on it while she held her knees. I looked down watching as my dick went in and out of her juicy pussy. She bounced and bounced putting in work as she wailed in pleasure. I pushed my toes into the floor to push up in her as she dropped down.

The hard fiberglass chair was painful on my back I

couldn't take no more of that shit after a good 10 minutes so we took it to the folding table.

"Sit up on there," I said.

She opened her legs when she sat down, I pulled her thighs towards me, so her ass could hang off the edge as she leaned back. I held her legs over my shoulder then threw this penis in the pussy. I began to dig and dig. She's wailed even louder, her titties bounced from each stroke, the table seemed loose rocking with us. But that didn't slow me down I kept on stroking. I stood up in it delivering pleasure, her hands were randomly grabbing shit as she moaned loud and her face expressions told me that she loved every second of it. Her breathing got exceedingly heavy and I stared at her as she tightly grasped the table. "I'm cummin ohhh I'm cummin"

I remain hitting the same spot

"Oh my Gosh, oh my Gosh!"

In seconds her body got brittle as soon as she let her nut loose I pushed my dick far up in her and held it inside while she screamed from the top of her lungs, quickly I covered her mouth.

She jumped off the table, on to her knees again and started sucking until I bust another nut.

003. FOGGY WINDOWS

On a Saturday night in my white clean impala I'm on the road riding through streets lights with my windows down, music banging enjoying the fall weather. I'm on my way to visit a beautiful friend of mine. We been fucking around for a year in some months but never committed to a relationship. We knew each other from social networks but happened to meet at a club in the Strip District. A simple "How you doing?" Led us into a long friendship with sexual benefits. The chemistry between us two was perfect, everything about her was flawless. The only thing that interfered our chances of being in a relationship was the distance of where we lived and our life schedules. I worked full time on the weekdays during the evening shifts. Passion attended a beautician school during the day, on top of that she lived an hour across town from me. She stayed with her mother who was strict about niggas being with her only daughter. She was grown but unfortunately, her mom wasn't comfortable with men coming in the house. The first time I picked Passion up to sleep over my apartment her mother wrote down my license plate and snapped a picture of my driver's license with the camera phone. Today I'm not bringing her home because riding there and back can take approximately an hour each way. She's worth every hour but today I wasn't in the mood to go back and forward.

"I'm outside" I sent her a text as soon as I pulled up to her house. I saw the curtains move in the window on the second floor. A few minutes later Passion walks out the house. She was a very atypical type of female; that's what made her more magnetic. She was way different than your average Keshia. She had an abnormal hairstyle, it was cut short on the left side of her head, on the right, she had long curly bouncy black weave. Her teeth were perfectly straight and white as snow, along with the nice teeth she had an admirable smile. She wore a SpongeBob letterman coat, black sweat pants, and a pair of brown cowgirl boots.

When she sat in the passenger seat, we leaned over towards each other with arms wide open to hug. She kissed my big lips then said,"Ohh baby, I missed youuuu."

The Orange street lights shined, the music played low as I reclined my chair. "I miss you too, how school?"

"School alright, they had me shave shaving cream off a balloon with a razor yesterday. I popped the first balloon, but I did good on the other ones. Maybe I'll cut your hair someday."

"Naw, you're not going to pop my head like you did them balloons.

She laughed shaking her head at my teasing. "I'll have you fresh and I popped only one balloon."

"I'm cool; I already got a permanent barber. But what else you been up to?"

"Nothing, when I come home from school I be in the house all day with my mom."

"Ohh, your mom, I'm scared of her. She don't like me huh?"

Her phone rang and she quickly pressed ignore. "She never said she don't like you. She's just strict about who I mess with. She seen me hurt before an she don't want me to go through the depression stage again."

"That's understandable; I ain't going to hurt you though. Hopefully one day I'll be all yours and you'll be mines."

Her long artificial eyelashes flapped as she turned her lips. "Hopefully, that's all on you I'm ready for a relationship."

"It's going to happen trust me. I got to focus on me before I add another person in my life; but I can definitely see myself being with you."

"Why could you see us together?"
"Why you got to ask this question?" I answered her question with a question.

"Because I want to know. So why could you see us together?"

I bit my bottom lip as I glanced directly in her big eyes. I thought hard and spoke slowly. "Ummmm because your personality is bomb, you're different I like your style, you got some fire pussy. Umm what else? Ummm I think we'll look good together plus you very attractive."

"Oh that sounds good. You just had to include sex." She giggled.

I rubbed her legs through the sweat pants. "I mean that pussy is very addictive. It stays soaked for me. Then you know how to fuck me the way I like to fuck. It's probably wet now huh?"

She shrugged her shoulders. "She might be, you got to find out yourself."

"Oh is that right?" I squinted my eyes. I slowly rubbed my right hand up her thighs, pulled her legs apart then reached for the crotch of the sweat pants. With the index, middle and ring fingers I rubbed the cotton from the sweats against her clit. She closed her eyes and nibbled on her pinky nail as she moaned softly with her mouth open.

"Mmmmmm here you go with your shit Tink Mmmmmm!"

I felt moisture seeking through her sweat pants as I continue to rub. "I can feel your juices coming through these sweats, that pussy must be wet as fuck."

Passion untied the string to the pants, snatched my wrist then slid my right hand down inside. Instantly my fingers become drenched and slippery. "Uh hum wet ain't it," she said.

I didn't say anything I began to flick her clit with the tip of my right index finger like I was pulling a gun. Her eyes were closed, mouth was wide open, her moans got louder and louder as she squirmed in the seat. While I caressed her body, I glanced over at the house and seen the curtains move. I got paranoid and pulled my hand out her sweat pants. "I think your Mom watching us, the curtains just moved."

"My mom sleep that's probably Bella, she's always in the window."

"Well your dog is nebby."

She giggled. "I know she's overprotective."

I turned the key on the turn emission. "We should get from in front of your house, I'm not trying to get based on by your raise."

"Okay, wait one minute I got to lock the front door." She stepped out the car, ran up the concrete steps then went inside the house. I immediately punched my password in my phone then scrolled down my timeline on Instagram. Most of the people on my timeline were going out tonight. A few of the ladies was looking stunting but some looked like mountain rats. As I double tapped on a number of ladies photos Passion made her appearance in the car.

"Sorry, I had to put the dog in the cage."

When the passenger door shut I switched the gear to drive.

"It's fine, do you know any spots we can

chill?"

"No, not off hand just find an alleyway."

We rode down a bumpy brick road going pass the projects, made a right at a stop sign at the bottom of the hill, and rode through a few streetlights then turned left on a random street in the middle of the hood. We cruised for another two minutes then found an alleyway with a dead end. The alley was pitch black, there was broken glass spread across the ground. To the left of the driver's side there was a boarded up abandoned house with graffiti on it that read "187 block." I parked the car then leaned my seat back. The green light from the radio was the only light that shined; the street light in the alley casually came on for a second then turned off.

It was an awkward moment when I parked; we both were silent for a few minutes. The tension was high I knew what she wanted; the expression on her face gave me signals that she wanted me inside her. She broke the silence as she kicked her boots off.

"What we doing? Are we getting in the back?"

"Yeah, go head. You first." She climbed between the seats then jumped in the back.

I pulled the passenger seat up then I followed

behind. "Is that pussy still wet for me?"

Passion didn't say much she slid her sweat pants halfway down her thighs. "Umm humm help me take these off."

I grabbed the end of her sweats and pulled them completely off. I had no choice but to eat her; I had an appetite as soon I glanced at that pussy. It was looking delicious and ready to eat. She took the SpongeBob jacket off then threw the jacket on the floor. She wore a white tank top that Read "LOVE" in huge black letters. On her shoulder blade going down her upper arm, she had a cheetah print tattoo.

She laid on her back and rested her head on the door. I kissed and sucked on her inner thighs slowly making my way up towards her sweet juices. The closer my lips approached the pussy the harder she breathed. I ran my wet tongue up to the destination then wrapped my lips around her clit. Working with a little bit of space in the car, I dropped to my knees so I could be comfortable. I filled my mouth with saliva and slid my tongue across as I sucked at the same time. I continued to smack her clit non-stop as juices dripped down my chin hairs.

"Mmmmmm oh God oh God!" She grabbed my head and moaned loudly.

I shook my face; I didn't lose focus or release my lips from around her clit. My face moved the surroundings of the pussy. I licked and sucking her clit shaking her outer areas with my face. In no time her body tightened, her legs got stiff, her moans were louder and her grip on the back of my head tightened.

"I'm cummming, I'm cummming!" She screamed as her legs shook like a seizure. I sucked every drop of her cum and continued to eat until she couldn't resist it. She pushed my forehead back and sat up on the seat, covering her pussy with both hands

"Stop stop stop! Owww stop! What the fuck are you doing to me?"

I smiled as I wipe my face off with a t-shirt on the floor. "You like that huh?"

"Boy you know I do, now give me some dick."

I kicked my Jordan's off, unbuckled my black leather belt and pulled my tight blue 501 jeans down pass my kneecaps. I got a hold of the condoms in the armrest, then I ripped the gold wrapping. I slid the rubber protector down my thick 8-inch black hard dick. It felt like my legs tangled in my pants as I tried to position myself to go in for the kill. I removed the pants off my right leg, so I could deliver a perfect stroke. I kept my left leg planted on the floor as I bended my right leg on the seat. I gripped her thighs and pulled her body towards my body, she opened her legs wide open. Her right foot was on the driver's headrest the other foot was in midair. I gradually stuck my dick inside and slowly stroked her as I leaned my upper body on top of hers. In and out I was constantly throwing my dick in her at a mid-steady pace

"Mmmmmm Mmmmmm Ohh Ohh Mmmmmm fuck this pussy!"

The pussy was tight, them juicy walls were squeezing the fuck out of penis. I felt myself moaning in between strokes. Her moans motivated me to fuck more aggressively, I sped the pace in my stroke. I lifted my upper body up then beat the fuck out of pussy. On the radio, Robin Thicke's "Blurred lines "played as she screamed over the music.

"Ohh shittt, oh mmm mmm! Fuck me fuck me!"

Few minutes into the session, I turned Passion

around, both of her knees were on the seat. She faced the back-passenger window. I was behind pushing her back down arching her back with the left; with the right I choked her by the neck while I stroked her with this black pipe. The blue tree air freshener jiggled on the rearview mirror, I could hear the shocks squeaking, every window was foggy from the hard breathing. I kept digging in her pushing every inch inside, she smeared the windows with her hands as she randomly touched shit. I was working her body drilling the back end. Sweat was dripping off my forehead onto her back.

It was extremely hot in the car and I stopped in the middle dicking her down. "Yo we got to roll these windows down."

I pulled my dick out then reached in the front to hit the power window switches. The cool breeze seeped through the cracks as I sat down to catch my breath. I wasn't near tired I just couldn't function when I'm hot.

"I came like three times." Passion took her tank top off and quickly broke the silence as she looked at me holding my hard dick in my hand.

"Damn I didn't even know. I probably tell you this all the time. But you got some bomb."

"You told me that an hour ago, when we was in front of my house."

"Can I ask you something?" She jumped on top of me sliding down my dick

"What?"

"Nevermind, I'll ask you when were done"

The front of her body was facing mine; I got a hold of her ass as she bounced on my dick like a pogo stick. I planted both feet on the floor and fucked her back. The pussy was overly wet I felt her juices dripping on my stomach. As she rode, I pushed up in her. Right as I was about to bust a nut a bright light flashed on us from a distance, immediately we paused knowing the cops were near.

004. HANDYMAN

Following the GPS to the next client's house in this hot stuffy van, it's 90 degrees outside and the A/C is barely blowing cool air. I complained several times to the manger regarding the automotive difficulties but again and again, they'll give me the run around and promise to repair the air conditioner bullshit. I sip at a cold fountain drink with the windows fully down to get as much air I can to stay cool. The GPS brought me to the street of my destination; I'm creeping down the street eyeballing the numbers on the houses, searching for 5809 on West Saint Clair. I pull in front of the house; the place seems to be a duplex, there's a brown picket fence surrounding a fresh cut lawn; I read the address on the assignment sheet to check what apartment the client lives in. I also check the resident name before I strap my tool belt on.

The sheet reads *"John Mason, apartment A"*

I open the gate, walk through the yard then go up the four concrete steps to apartment A. I ring the doorbell once then wait a few seconds, not even a whole minute later I hear the door slowly open as I gaze around and watch a red 2015 Chevy truck pull behind my van. I turn my head to greet the customer opening the door

"Hi... Hi...How...You...You... Doing...Doing..." I stutter as I surprisingly get caught off guard staring at a beautiful naked brown woman standing in the door way, her titties are huge and perfect they have to be a 36DD, her nipples and stomach are pierced, she has tattoos of roses and a rose vine on the side of her right thigh that goes up her rib cage. She pulls the door shut forcefully as she apologizes.

"Oh my God Sorry, I thought you was my boyfriend."

"It's okay ma'ma..."

"I forgot you were coming." she screams from the other side of the door.

The guy who parked behind my van steps on the first two concrete steps with confusion on his face as he catches the tail end of the situation. "Hey what's going on NOW." he says with a deep tone in his voice as he takes his last step on the porch.

I am indecisive about telling him what just happened. *Should I flat out just tell him I seen his wife naked or should I tell him his wife had some nice titties?* "Well, hey sir you must be Mr. Mason."

"Yeah, why my girlfriend slammed the door on you?" he asks.

"Oh, um she thought I was you and answered the door butter ball."

"Butter ball? What you mean?" He questions super confused.

"She came to the door naked, I guess you were suppose to get some" I joke.

"Ha ha Yeah, we're making an attempt to have a baby, we fuck every chance we get. She wants a baby bad."

"Well homie you got to handle that; I have another customer house down the street. I can come back in an hour when I'm finished with them, I'll give you time to plant your seed."

"Aww man I really appreciate that man, thanks." He's grateful as he reaches for my hand to shake.

"No, problem."

"I probably won't be here when you come back, I'll be sure she'll have clothes on." He looks back at me before opening the screen door.

"I would hope so, ay man enjoy."

I get back in my steaming hot van then call the following client, whose appointment was originally at 1:30; it's approximately 11:45 am just a little before noon I really hope Mr. Tort won't mind me rearranging the schedule

The phone rings once then went straight to voicemail; I don't want to seem weird by sitting in the front of the couple's house, I have a feeling they are peeking out the window waiting for me to pull off. Just in case they were I drive a few blocks down the street and park in front an elementary school. I call Mr. Tort again and still didn't get an answer. After 15 minutes of waiting; now I'm frustrated and bitchy like a woman on her period, I'm sweating bullets and complaining to myself as I feel sweat running down my spine, the radio playing the same shit which isn't making anything better, on top of that dude not answering his phone.

"FUCK THIS STUPID ASS VAN, I'M NOT WORKING TOMORROW IF I HAVE TO DRIVE THIS SHIT. "It's supposed to be 98 degrees tomorrow along with the humidity, that's the apartment upstairs from the devil's.

Fifteen minutes go past; I can't take sitting it this van for another second. I turn the key in the ignition then make a stop at a nearby gas station. They have a touchscreen menu with variety of foods from hot to cold, I'm obsessed with the chicken tenders; nice and crispy white tender meat and their fries are delicious as well, you can eat them without ketchup or dipping sauce. I pay for my food then sit in the lounging area and use the WIFI to save gigs on my Sprint plan.

Time is racing and I'm full, I feel fat like a walking blimp, my stomach is sticking out but that's fine with me, the ladies love guys with bellies. The client lives five minutes away, I drive to their place. When I pull in front of the house, I notice the truck isn't there and the gate is propped open. The gate squeaks as I push it to enter the yard. I wipe the sweat off my forehead then knock on the door. Seconds of waiting she answers the door with a bright beautiful smile on her face, she has a smile on her face as if her man made her cum a thousand times. This time she isn't naked and has on short black shorts and white tank top

"Hey, come in!"

I pull the screen door open then step in the house with my tool belt wrapped around my waist.

"Where do you need new cables at?" I ask.

"In the basement, we just got the basement remodeled, We put new carpet and furniture down there. I guess it's John's little man cave. Would you be able to mount the TV on the wall?"

"Yes, I can, every man has to have a man cave. Especially for football games, you might not see him during football season."

"Oh God, I barely see him now."

I raise my eyebrows and shrug my shoulders, *that's none of my business*. I follow her to the basement door in the kitchen. "Your boyfriend must be a busy man."

"He is, I'm here lonely most of the time, it's like he's only here to sleep, we don't even have sex."

I spot the 40-inch TV boxed on the floor laying against the molded wall, the basement smelled like sour clothes; this is definitely, what I wasn't expecting the man cave to look like.

Before the conversation goes elsewhere, I change the subject because the way she is talking and eyeballing me down I'm thinking she needs some chocolate dick in her life. "I'm guessing you want the television mounted right here on this wall?"

"Yes, right there," she nods standing with her hand on her hip.

"Okay, aww dammit! You know what?"

"What?"

"I forgot to grab my drill out the truck."

"Go ahead! Would you like a can of soda?"

"No thank you, if you have ice water I would appreciate that." I request.

"Okay, I'll get that for you." She smiles happy for conversation. She follows me up the stairs then follows me down when I return with the drill. This woman talks my ear off. I drink half of the cup of water then I began the project. I kneel to my knees and drill a hole in the wall, just enough to fit the cable wires through.

"Do you have any kids?" She picks up her game of twenty-one questions.

"Yes, two," I answer trying to be polite. I pull the wires out then slip it through the hole in the wall.

"What do you have a girl and a boy" she guessed.

"No, two girls," I answer not even looking at her.

"Awww how old are they?" She stands in front of me forcing me to look at her as we make small talk.

"They're four and five."

"Oh, God I know they keep you busy."

"Yeah, they do."

"I've been attempting to get pregnant for a month or two."

I chuckle not surprised by her openness. "I see, your boyfriend, already told me."

"The problem is that his penis won't get hard for me or it will be hard for a minute then it will get soft."

That was a first. I search for the correct response and come up blank every time, so I resort to just an, "Oh okay."

"At the beginning of our relationship we used to fuck all the time, he'll come in the house fuck me in the shower or bend me over the couch, we would do it in every room."

I stand up grabbing my measuring tape and pencil trying not to think about this woman's desperation. "That's bad."

"I know, and the crazy part I never had an orgasm."

"You never had an orgasm? How long have you to been together?" I question her while I measure and mark where to drill for the TV mount.

"Never had one, we been together for two years almost three, Have you ever made a woman have an orgasm?"

I stretch the measuring tape against the wall and mark where I'll drill the holes. "Oh yeah, plenty of time, I'm all for pleasing a woman," I say with confidence in my voice. As I mark the last dot she reaches for my measuring tape.

"Let me see!"

I don't have clue why she wants the measuring tape, but I hand it over to her. She stretches the tape out; then lets it roll back in. "What's that silly look on your face for?"

"No reason." I say now intrigued.

"Mmmmm, how big is your dick?" She asks stretching the tape again.

"I don't know." I answer even though I know the size of my dick. She approaches me reaching for my tool belt.

"Well, let's see Mr. Handy Man." The tool belt drops to my ankles as I loosen the side and she drops to her knees.

"Oh, damn you're serious" I'm saying as I glance down at her ripping my pants loose.

"Mmmm hummm..."

My dick is hard just from the conversation earlier, but I wasn't aware that things would escalate this far. She pulls my dick out the grey boxer briefs before admiring my dick's size.

"Wow, you have a huge dick." She stretches the measuring tape next to my black thick and long dick. Looking down at her beautiful face next to my dick I am hoping she'll put her mouth around it. "Sheesh! Eight inches just about nine" she speaks in a celebratory tone before kissing the tip of my dick.

"I might need this in my life!" She grabs my dick tight from the middle then licks around my shaft. I'm biting my bottom lip still not believing what's happening. She holds my dick with her finger tips rolling her tongue up and down each side of it; making my dick extremely wet. I kick my tool belt to the side, so I can spread my legs further to keep my balance as she puts her mouth around my dick. She begins to suck while she strokes my dick with passion at the same time.

"Mmmm suck that shit, mmmm just like that mmmmm, keep going! Her head moves back and forward, the sounds of her slurping turn me on even more. "Mmmm suck that dick."

It feels so good that I'm about to nut in her mouth in minutes, before I can bust I stop her; pushing her off my dick.

"Hold on, hold on babe what you trying to do to me, let me take my pants off and you lay over there." I demand.

"Okay," she agrees with wet lips.

"Let me taste you now."

"Mmm okay, where you want me to sit?"

"Right, there is fine."

She lays on the brand new burgundy couch and slides her gym shorts and panties off.

"Spread your legs open and rub your pussy." I demand.

She opens her legs wide and rubs her index and middle fingers side to side against her clit, she's wailing loud as she pleases herself, the pussy sounds wet as fuck! I can see her juices pouring from the pussy down to her asshole.

As I watch, my mouth gets watery like a starving man with a juicy cheeseburger in front of his face. I kneel down it front of her and kiss on her thighs; I would usually tease a woman to get her worked up, but she warmed herself up so fuck the foreplay. I wrap my lips around her clit as I build up saliva in my mouth, I slide my tongue back and forward across her clit while I suck gently.

"OH MY GOD mmmmmm," she wails.

I'm eating her pussy like there's no tomorrow, my face is completely wet. While I slob her pussy down, I build more saliva in my mouth to let it roll from her pussy lips down to her ass to make her asshole wet enough to plug my middle finger in. As I suck and lick I wiggle my finger inside her asshole, her body jerks and her moans go to another level.

"Ohhhh shit, oh shit," she wails.

With the opposite hand, I stick my index finger in her mouth to get the tip moist. I then grab hold of her left breast then rub her nipple all in the same time, I'm devouring her pussy and fingering her ass.

"OH YES, YES MMMMMMM!"

She's moaning nonstop.

I remove my lips from her pussy then remove my shirt, I push her legs back to the back of the couch with one hand holding both ankles, with the other hand I slowly aim the head of my dick to the opening of her pussy. Her pussy was so damn wet my whole thumb got soak as I plug my dick in her. I push my dick deep in her and stretch her walls with my thick dick; seem like she lost her breath as I began to stroke her spirit. Her mouth is wide open, her eyes are rolling to the back of her head and her hands are all over the place. I let go of her ankle and lay her legs over my shoulders, I reach for her throat and choke her while throw this dick inside her.

"Take this dick, take this dick," I say as she moans from the penetration. The pussy feels amazing, tight and wet; just how I love it, I find myself moaning as well

"Mmmh you feel this dick in you?"

Her expression shows me that she was enjoying every moment. "Yes, yes, yes!"

I'm stroking her pussy and talking shit. "You feel this dick all deep in you?"

 "Yes, yes, yes Ooh goodness!"

We stopped and switch positions I sat on the edge of the couch, she climbs on top of me and slides down on my dick. She then wraps her arms around my neck and starts grinding on my dick. I'm squeezing her soft ass and smacking it as I lift my hips up to fuck her back. Her titties are bouncing in my face, she tilted her head back as she moaned out loud, "I'm about to cum, I'm about to cum," she screamed.

I continue to force my dick in her as her wet pussy pulls my dick.

"I'm cumming, I'm cumming"

Her body tightens up as she screams from the top of her lungs. I hold down on her ass and push my dick further in her to make her climax harder.

Minutes after sitting on my dick, she gives me head

then I bust a nut all over her titties.

Time is ticking I still have an appointment at 1:30, we just fucked for 45 minutes and I haven't really done anything but fixed her body.

"Wow that was great" she says.

When I finished the job I fucked her one more time in the kitchen before I leave, after that I never seen her in two years until I spotted her with the boyfriend at Walmart pushing a cart with a toddler inside. The baby looks just like me YIKES!

005. NETFLIX AND CHILL

Many Ways to Eat

"I can help the next person in line!" The clerk yelled from behind the glass rolling her eyes with eyelashes thicker than a pigeon's wing.

"Hello, I can help whoever next in line!" She yelled again in my direction. I couldn't snap out of it, I was mesmerized by the beautiful brown skin, big booty girl standing in front of me! She was medium height, with curly red weave and beautiful brown skin, she had high cheek bones with a smile that would make your heart melt butter left overnight on the stove! It could have been all in my head just because I couldn't take my focus off of her, but I'm sure every eye in the place was focused on her too and I wasn't about to let anyone scoop her before I did! Politely I approached her with confidence, threw a compliment her way, which made her laugh, introduced myself then pow I was typing her number into my phone. I didn't consider myself a player but I'm more than confident in myself and it was never hard for me to rope in the females.

Later on that night we started texting and it led to us texting and talking throughout the week. By the end of the week all the talking and texting paid off because, we had plans on seeing each other. Instead of my normal game of asking when I could come over or when she was coming to see me, I figured she was worth more than that and decided to take her out. I had enough confidence to know that when given the choice at the end of the night to stay over or go, she'd choose to stay and females just like males know before their date arrives if they're going to let a nigga fuck or not!

I wasn't into taking women to the movies on the first date because it's not a good way to get to know a person, but Bad Grandpa was supposed to be good, so dinner and a movie sounded cool.

"That movie was not what I expected it to be, I didn't like how it ended but I still had a good time." She giggled as the two of us exited the theater.

"Swear, the previews hyped the movie up," I agreed with her, "but I'm glad you enjoyed my presence cause I sure as he'll enjoyed yours! Next time we're going somewhere fun. Have you ever been to Latitude 40? "

"No, I've never been there, but I'm glad there's going to be a next time," she responded stepping into the car with a huge grin on her face.

"Of course, beautiful," I slickly tried to hurry up and turn on the car, so we could get some heat.

"Whoooo hurry up and turn the heat on!" She blew into her folded hands. "It's freezing!"

"I know give it a few minutes to heat up."

"Okay, where we going? Your house or mine?" She looked down at her phone. I could tell she was nervous, but she said exactly what I wanted to hear!

My thoughts instantly switched to fucking her

and I grinned instantly knowing she wanted the dick. "I don't know it's up to you."

"My place is a mess I tore the house up trying to find something to wear. We can go to your house."

"That's fine, you drink I got Henny left over from last weekend?"

"Oh no I don't drink brown liquor it makes me evil, I'll be ready to fight you once I'm drunk."

"Naw I'm not trying get my ass whooped, I got wine you can sip on too, we don't need violence on the first date." I laughed.

"No, we don't, I wouldn't hurt you tho." She smirked and looked at me with her beautiful brown eyes.

About 15 minutes later, we arrived at my house and sat in the car for probably around 5 minutes trying to soak up as much heat as possible before stepping out into the cold air. "You ready," I asked. 'We goin' make a run for it!"

"Yeah I'm ready I think! But we gon have to cuddle when we get inside so I can get warm again!"

"That's cool with me," I said swinging the door open and running over to her side to open hers! I quickly entered the key into the keyhole, opened the door and stepped into my nice warm living room! I flicked the lights on and kicked off my shoes. "Do you want a tour?"

"Sure," she smiled unbuttoning her leather jacket.

"Well this is the living room, I'm hardly in here."

"Why is it so clean in here? I wouldn't expect that from a man; did you pick the colors and the furniture?"

"Yeah!" I smiled at the fact that she was impressed.

She twisted her lips in disbelief. "A woman had to help you."

"Nah, I designed everything myself I picked the furniture, I painted the walls, laid new carpet down, I had to make the apartment feel homely." In the kitchen, I reached inside the cupboard to grab the wine glasses. I opened the bottle then poured a glass for the both of us. I handed her glass to her and continued the tour showing her the kitchen, bathroom and spare bedroom finally ending the tour in the bedroom. She sat on the queen-sized bed holding the glass of wine while I switched the batteries from the DVD remote to the cable box remote. I changed the channel then sat next to her and watched as she browsed through Instagram, sliding her thumb upwards on the phone screen.

"I'm bout to order a movie or something for us to watch, you staying with me tonight?"

"I can do that, you got somethin I can sleep in?"

"Yeah I'll grab you somethin."

"Don't be tryna hit nothin either cause it's not going down," she said giving me the side eye.

"That wasn't even on my mind, I just want to

relax and cuddle with my new friend so you cool babe, I'm not going to try anything." I sipped my wine lying through my teeth! I knew more than anything if a female even mentions sex before a nigga even tries then sex is somewhere in the near future! I went in the drawer and got her some hoop shorts and t-shirt to wear. "Do you need me to leave the room while you change?"

"No, you're fine; I don't have anything you haven't seen before." She sat the glass down on the floor then stood up.

"I won't look," I said noticeably peeking through the cracks of my fingers. She laughed as she kicked her Uggs off and pushed her leggings down revealing her thick thighs and her round and plump ass that was swallowing her red thong. I bit my bottom lip and smiled enjoying every bit of what I was seeing. "I'm not trying to make you uncomfortable by staring but you have the most beautiful body, I bet you taste good too." Abruptly I spoke letting my thoughts slip out of my mouth.

"Um mmm look at you being fresh!" She threw the shorts at my face before continuing. "I don't need these, I sleep in my panties I'm sure I can trust you'll keep your hands to yourself anyway sir." She smiled climbing into bed.

I removed my clothes too stripping down to my boxers and socks, sat my wine glass on the nightstand and turned the lights out. "I'll keep my hands to myself." I lied again. "So what movie you wanna order?"

"You don't have to order a movie; we can just watch something that's on cable, other than sports."

"We'll you can find what you want to watch." I handed her the remote while folding my pillow so I was comfortable. Once I got situated she laid her head on my chest, and I wrapped my arm around her body pulling her in closer. She flipped through the channels for a few seconds then eventually selects a program to watch.

As we cuddled we hardly paid any attention to what was on TV, exchanged our thoughts and had deep conversations about our past relationships and goals we wanted to achieve in the future. Eventually after talking for a while naturally, I had to incorporate sex into the conversation.

"So what's your sexually fantasy?"

She glanced upwards. "Umm... I don't know, I never had sex on a beach that might be one of them, what's yours?"

"You want to have sand stuck in your butt?" I laughed imagining how uncomfortable she would be.

"You're goofy."

"That sounds fun tho, I want to fuck in the

143

library on top of books, since it's a place where you're supposed to be quiet. I want to do it on the plane in the small bathroom too though that seems fun too."

She twisted up her face amused. "In the library though? You're crazy, what if she's loud?"

"I'll cover her mouth if she moans, I want to eat a woman while she's driving too. I never did that with anybody before and I NEED to make it happen sometime soon!"
She sat up and reached for the wine glass on the nightstand then took a sip.

"Is that even possible? How would she even be able to focus on the road? "

"I don't know how but it's possible."
"You must really like to give head."
"I don't mind doing it, I love seeing a woman's body reactions when I'm licking and sucking."
"Ohh stop we have to get off this conversation please. I'm already sexually frustrated."

My phone rang in the interrupting our moment and I ignored the call. "Why are you frustrated?" I asked.

"I haven't had sex in eight months!"

"Eight months... oh fucckk no... I'd be out here evil as hell, cussing random people out and shit. I would help you out but you said no sexual activities. When was the last time you got some head?"

"I got head last month by my best friend."

"At least you got a little action, is your friend a dude?" I did a double take backing up the conversation.

"No, she's a girl, don't judge me." She giggled.

"You have to tell me about this, I'm not going judge you."

"I'm not going to tell you the whole story, we was just curious. Well I was, but she's always been gay."

"Some chick told me that girls eat pussy better than men, is that true?"

"Mannnnn hell yeah! I mean I had some guys who were good, but the way she ate me was unforgettable! "

"Is that right, I bet she's not better than me. I'd have you changing your mind real quick if I tasted that." I reached for her inner thighs rubbing my hand inward.

"I wouldn't mind you tasting it, but this is our first time together and I already know if I let you eat it, I'm going to want dick and I don't wanna go there! Soooo You can just explain to me how you'd eat it." I positioned myself between her legs and as if it was instinct, she pushed my forehead back. "What are you doing?"

"I'mma demonstrate how I would start, don't worry I'm not gonna touch you, now lay back." I kissed her stomach before continuing my narration. "First I'd tease you to get your body worked up, the more I tease you the more anxious you'd be for my tongue to cross your clit."

My tongue ran circles around her belly button then moved down to her pelvic area and licked and kissed each side leaving a wet mess. The story was fiction, but the teasing was real because she let a loud moan escape her lips. I opened her legs wide then placed my lips on her inner thighs; gently I scraped my teeth against her soft brown skin and licked at the same time. Gradually I made my way up towards her pussy, the closer I got the louder her moans got, I felt her body getting weak as she was getting closer and closer to where I wanted her to be. Finally giving in she cuffed my head and smashed my head into her pussy.
I kissed the lips of her pussy while glancing dead into her eyes, the expression on her face was begging for oral attention. I kissed her pussy again then I wrapped my lips around her clitoris, it was tender like a gummy bear, I built up saliva in my mouth then slid my tongue back and forth across her wet pussy.

Back and forth, my wet tongue smacked against her clit at a slow pace while I sucked gently, as

I moved my tongue, I sucked air into my mouth to bring sensitivity to the clitoris. Gripping a handful of my sheets in her palms, her stomach sunk in and out as she inhaled and exhaled. I consistently ran my tongue across the same spot causing her to wiggle and squirm letting me know this motion was bringing her pleasure.

I applied more pressure then sped the pace of my tongue to be experimental; as her moans got louder, I stuck two fingers inside her pussy curling my index and ring finger upwards rubbing against the upper walls. I sucked and licked her clit while I rubbed against the g-spot throwing her into pure ecstasy. She grabbed hold of the headboard pulling on the bar as she gripped the back of my head pushing it into her pussy and moving up and down as if she was riding my face.

"Oh shit shit shit," she moaned as her juices leaked down my chin, dripping onto the sheets.

"I'm cumming," she announced as her legs locked tight around my head. I shook my face in the pussy with my mouth still on the clit.

"Ohhhh shit, shiittt," she wailed as I kept sucking and licking nonstop. She pushed the back of my head strongly smothering my face in the pussy until her legs got flimsy and her nut was all on my lips.

When she finished cumming she laid flat on the bed with her legs open, she was useless and drained. I slowly licked her clit with the tip of my wet tongue giving her a chance to get herself together.

"What are you doing to me?" she asked

moaning. I ignored her question taking in a mouthful of her pussy. I wasn't nearly done my goal was to make her feel as though she was going to pass out. Starting from the perineal body, which is between the vagina and the anus, I ran my tongue upwards to slide it inside the pussy, I opened her lips with both hands to expose the clit. I licked upward sliding my tongue against the clit, also using my top lip.

A few minutes into the attempt to make her cum again I switched the technique. I gripped her ankles and pushed her legs back, I slid my tongue across her clit several times, slowing then speeding up the pace like my tongue was a vibrator. I held both ankles with the left hand to free my right hand, so I was able to stick my fingers in the pussy in an arched form. Side to side I moved my index and middle fingers at a fast motion. Moaning loudly and balling up her fist, she began banging on the mattress yelling.

"Keep going keep going."

Even though the veins in my forearm were burning I didn't stop, I kept the fingers going and my tongue moving.

"Ohhh fuckkk!" Her body got stiff as she released again, I dropped her legs and continued to eat. She began to crawl back pushing my head.

"Oh my God, Stop stop stop!"

I kissed her pussy softly as she attempted to get herself together. I pulled my dick out the slit of my boxers and reached under the bed for the box of condoms. I removed a condom and slid it over my rock-hard dick. I climbed over top of her, and attempted to stick it in.

"I can't do this, it's our first time being together." She responded, pushed me off of her and turned her back towards me.

I guess she was serious about no sex, I thought to myself. "Oh we'll," I shrugged my shoulders, turned my back, and went to sleep.

006. SEX ON THE CLOCK

"Bye!"
"Enjoy your day."
"See you tomorrow Mr. Smith."
"Hi!"
"Bye!"

It's 4:45pm on a Monday evening I'm at work, putting in my hours 3 to 11. I'm in my white security shirt with the silver badge, navy blue tie and navy-blue dress pants. My old butter Timbs was still fresh with a few scuffmarks.

Behind the desk, I'm standing next to the monitors, in a good mood speaking to the people as they come and go. This beautiful petite red bone woman approached the front desk. She has the most attractive smile on the face of the planet. What made her smile more engaging was the small gap in her front teeth. She had long black natural hair. Nothing fancy she wore khaki pants and a black leather jacket for the cold fall weather outside. She has on a pair of black 95 Air Maxes. As soon as she gets close to the counter, the work phone rings and I quickly answer. "Security, Darren speaking."
The supervisor from the account department called to confirm that he's having a new employer coming in.

"Hey, Darren this is Steve. I have a lady by the

name of Carla Keys coming in around five." I glance at the girl, guessing she is Carla.

"Okay, I think I have your person here."

"Oh, great she's early."

As the fine red bone stands in front of the desk with patience, I briefly put the account supervisor on hold. I lick my lips to get them moist before greeting her. "Are you Carla?"

"Yes," with a soft tone in her voice she answers.

"Oh, ok you came just in time. Your supervisor is on the phone now."

She smiles showing her small gap. "What a coincidence."

"I know." Before I can say more the account supervisor interrupts.

"Let her know I'll be down there in a few minutes."

"Okay will do." I hang up and finally give Carla my full attention. "Your supervisor on his way to come get you, can you sign in for me?"

She grabs the pen then writes her full name, date, and time in the login book. After she jots her information, I give her a white card. I smile while handing her the card. *"I should swerve on her gorgeous ass"* I think to myself not dropping my smile. My thoughts didn't mean shit cause my heart nerves, shut my thinking process down. It's her first day I didn't want her to feel uncomfortable either.

"What is this card for?" She asks holding the card in her hand.

I still smile realizing I didn't tell her much because I am way too busy checking her out. "Oh sorry, that's a temporary card that gives you access to the elevators and cafeteria. Your supervisor should be giving you a tour soon."

"Okay, why you keep smiling so much?"

I smile some more displaying my one dimple on the right side of my face. "I can't help but to smile when there's an attractive woman in my presence."

"Aww, thanks you're attractive yourself."

In the middle of exchanging compliments, her supervisor interrupts again walking toward the desk.

"Thanks hun, well there goes your supervisor Steve right there."
"Okay, nice meeting you, what's your name"
"Darren but everyone calls me Tink."
"My name is..."
"Carla, I already know your name love. Enjoy your first day." I interrupt reminding her.

She returns my smile before walking away. "You do the same"

"I will."

"Carla Keys?" Steve interrupts my daydreaming and shakes her right hand.

"Yes that's me."

"I'm Steve Amero, I'll be training you today. Did he give you a card?"

"Yes," she nods flashing Steve the card I gave her.

"Good follow me."

"Thanks man," Steve finally thanks me as the two walk away from the desk.

"No problem. Y'all take it easy. Don't work her too hard," I joke standing behind the desk watching her as she walks down the hallway.

"What the fuck you lookin' at?" My co-worker interrupts my staring just as he's finishing his rounds.

"Oh, damn! She bad, I hope you got them digits." He spoke as soon as Carla glances back.

"NO!! MAN GET YOUR FAT ASS ARM OFF ME!"

My co-worker Brad, cool as fuck we be cutting up all day and every day. He brown skin with Bobby Valentino curls, and a cut. He's one of them fat dudes who's fresh, and always dresses nice to impress the ladies. He's hell of funny, personality is humorous. People love this nigga.

"You must've been shook, my fat ass would've been all over that." Brad sat in the chair smiling thinking about Carla.

"Yeah right nigga, you don't have juice like that. But I'm taking my time it's her first day."
"So, what the fuck that means?" He twists his face in confusion.

"She's definitely bad, I'm not trying to look thirsty."
"Don't let me see her alone, I'll show you how get on woman little nigga, big nigga like me turn chicks out." Brad slowly stands up then pulls change out his pocket

"Alright, whatever nigga." I laugh entertained by his nonsense.

"You want something from the vending machine?"
"Yeah, a Mountain Dew"
He gives me a wild stare as I stare at him in confusion.

"What now?"
"The money for your pop."
"I thought you was getting it."
"I am, with your money."

"Get me some onion rings too." I sigh in defeat before pulling two dollars out my pocket.

Throughout the night after work, Carla ran through my mind.

Tuesday back on the shift I see her again, she walks pass the desk waving with a big smile on her face. My heart beats like snare drum in a parade and I can't help it. I smile back, biting my bottom lip and of course Brad interrupts my daydreaming.

"Yo, you should've said something."

"I am, swear when I see her next time I'm going to."

"You better, or I'm going to say something for you."

"Yo, don't do that man. I'll get her myself. Ahh you trying to pitch in on some food?" I pull out the menu from Pizza Parma.

"Yeah, after I do my round."

"Alright…"

A hour passes we buy a large pepperoni pizza, two whole Italian hoagies and a dozen of hot wings with blue cheese and ranch on the side. Behind that desk all on camera we demolish this grease dripping delicious food. In minutes, half of the food is gone. Brad sits in the chair acting like a drunk, rubbing his big belly.

"Damn that shit was fire." He's the first to speak.

"I know I don't even feel like doing my rounds." While I stand to my feet with a full stomach, I see Carla from far distance walking down the hall. I tap Brad and smile. "Oh shit, here she come!"

I wipe my mouth then I pop a peppermint on my tongue to get the onion smell out. It seemed like shit was going in slow motion as she gets closer and closer. I feel my nose sweating cause I'm nervous. In reality this would be a homerun in the ball park for me, if it was any other chick but somehow this woman got my nuts.

"Hey, Tink or should I say Darren." She steps to the desk as I wipe the sweat off my nose.

"Tink cool," I respond acting shy smiling at her.

"Steve sent me up here to get my picture taken for my own access card." She smiles and hands over her white card.

The pressure was turned up to 100 as I hear the chair behind me squeaking loudly to the point that I can't hear myself talk. I look back and see Brad making faces, pointing at me trying to get her attention. I give him this annoyed face mouthing, "What the fuck are you doing dawg?

"Yo, fuck it. This nigga is scared to talk to you. Since he met you he been over here talking about you." He wipes the crumbs off his white shirt and goes for it and to my surprise, Carla's smile widens.

"Is that right, Mr. Security guard?"

"We're getting the fair one after work." I glance over at Brad trying not to show my embarrassment.

"She's talking to you." Brad laughs not intimidated by my threats.

"I didn't want to say anything too soon cause you just started." I bite my bottom lip again explaining myself to Carla.

"Yeah, right this nigga was beyond scared." Brad stands up to his feet then put his forearm on my shoulder.

"Was he? Tink You don't got to be scared of me."

"I wasn't shook through." I push Brad arm off me and shake my head in denial.

"Yes, he was." Brad interrupts not letting it go.

"Yo, shut up man! Damn. Matter fact

where's the camera and the key to the photo room? "

"The camera in the bottom cabinet on the right." Brad pulls the keys out his pocket and I grab the two items, then step out the door.

"I'll be back. Come on Carla." She follows me to the backroom where it's finally me and her alone. As I'm getting the camera ready she stands next to me staring at me with a smile on her face.

"Where you from?" She leans against the wall.
"Manchester, but I live on The Hill. What about you?"
"I'm from East Liberty. I live behind Peabody High School."
"Oh, do you know Parren and his brother?"
"Yeah, those my niggas!"
"That's why you look so familiar, I think I seen you at one of their cookouts."
"Yeah, I'm always at their cookouts. They're like family."

"Are you ready?" Finally, I ask fixing the camera.

She removes her jean jacket and sets it on the table. "Where do you want me to stand?"
"Stand in front of the screen." I point to the projector screen on the wall.

She stands in front of the screen as I shut my

left eye to focus the camera.

"Fuck your fine as hell." I snap the shot smiling.

"Thank you," her smile can't get any wider at this point.

I snap at least 12 shots. She looks at them all but doesn't like neither one of them. To impress her I have to snap more shots. I show her the photos again. Being picky she says, "Uggg I don't know, it's out of this one and that one."

"Which one you want I think they're all beautiful pics of you."
I flip back and forward showing both pictures.
"Thanks, I'll take ahhhhhh that one."
"Are you sure?"
"No no, I want that one for sure."
"Alright."
Whenever we finish with the shoot we go back to the desk. Unsurprisingly Brad is knocked out sleeping like a newborn baby right in front of the camera. "YO, WAKE UP"
Slobber leaks down his chin as he jumps up startled.
"What, What, What!"
Carla stood in the front of the desk as I make her card. We both laugh at Brad as he comes out his sleep. It didn't take more than two minutes to finish her card. I walk around the desk then walk with her to the account management room. Before she goes in we exchange numbers.

Every day for two weeks we talk and text. She even chills with me in my hideout spot in the building on her 30-minute lunch breaks. Things were cool between us. Brad got fired for pulling a no call no show two days in the row. There was a new person who worked with me who was friends with the boss. Dude was the biggest snitch in the world.

On a Thursday night I'm in my hideout spot with the lights out. I'm on my phone listening to music. My hideout spot is a conference room with big glass windows on the 10th floor. Through the glass windows, I can see the pretty skyline of Downtown Pittsburgh up close and personal.

Just chilling sitting in the comfortable chair, with my feet up on the conference table. Carla texts me.

"Where you at? You're not in the front."
"I'm on the 10th floor."
"I'll be there in 5 minutes"
"Alright!"

Less than five minutes later she opens the door. I take my foot off the table as she walks in, to sit on my lap. "How's work?" I ask placing my arms around her body.

"It's alright just boring, I couldn't wait to see you, I left a couple minutes early."

"That's what's up, I didn't even get a kiss though. See you're fuckin up."

She stands up then sits back down, facing me face to

face. I grab her little ass as our lips touches. Her lips tasted like birthday cake lip-gloss. Our tongues smack each other like a sword fight. I can't control myself; my dick is hard as a crowbar, leaving a long shadow in my pants. She wraps her arms around my neck and whispers in my ear I feel something poking me. I grab her ass tighter, pulling her into my dick so she can feel it a bit more through her khakis pant. "Oh, do you..."

"Mmmmm please don't start with me Tink."

We kiss some more, I kiss under her neck. Then I run my wet tongue up, going towards her earlobe. The city lights, headlights and brake lights shine on us through the wide windows as we make out. She moans as I continue to caress her body. I lift her shirt up to suck on her nipples. Her nipples are light brown, it was the size of Mike and Ikes. When I suck on them they feel as if I'm sucking on gummy bears. In the middle of going to second base, she puts her index finger on my forehead to push me off her.

"I can't do this, I gotta go back to work." She interrupts our moment.
My hormones are let down.
"Oh oh okay, damn you got my dick hard."

She scoots back just enough to pull my 8-inch black curled dick out. That's big, I don't know about you."

I bite my bottom lip as she strokes. The feeling of her beating my dick has me ignoring whatever she was saying.

"That feels good," I groan.

She stops beating, and then struggles to slip my dick in my boxer hole.

"Hummm, babe I got to go. I'll handle that when I come back on my 15 minutes break."

"Alright babe."

She stands up and pulls me up off the chair to walk with her to the door. I geet behind her with my arms around her body as we slowly head towards the door.

"Only if you knew what's going through my mind."

As we get to the door, she turns around then kisses me. "What's on your mind?"

"Nothing you'll see."

"Whatever I'll see you in an hour."

Our lips touch, then she exits the room. I do another round through the building. After handling my business, I duck off to my hideout spot. 20 minutes of sitting being bored scrolling down my Twitter timeline. I hear a knock at the door. I don't know who it is, I don't know if the new dude snitched and have the manager here or not. After a certain time, I usually leave the desk, but he doesn't know that. I REALLY DON'T KNOW. Most of the time Carla calls. So I'm clueless.

The door opens slowly, through the crack the hallway lights got wider in the room. Carla steps in, shutting the door behind her. "We got 15 minutes."

I'm sitting in the chair as she walks towards me aggressively. "15 minutes for what?"

She doesn't say anything she sits on me, sitting face to face then unbuttons my white work shirt. Kissing on my neck, she whispers in my ear. "I want you to fuck me, stand up."

She jumps up off my lap, I stand to my feet. She reaches for my belt buckle yanking it to unbuckle the belt; she unbuttons my pants then zips my zipper down. My pants fall straight to the floor. With both hands she gets a hold of my plain black boxers, forcefully sliding my underwear to the floor along with my pants. My dick jumps out hard like jack in the box.

Carla falls to her knees and put her mouth on my penis. She wasn't bullshitting that neck was get thrown like a baseball. Her mouth is wet and warm. She works her mouth and uses her hand at the same time. Her saliva drips down her chin onto my boxers. I grab the back of her head, pushing her forehead into my abs.

Not even two minutes of getting the head I tap

her shoulder. "Get up and Take those pants off."

She stands up then slides her pants down to her boots. "Do you want me to take these off too?"

"Yeah, take all of that off." Luckily I have condoms in my pocket cause the way I was feeling, we would be fucking raw. I grab the condom out my pocket as she removes her boots.

I pick her petite body up from the floor. Then I sit Carla on the wood grain conference table. Her legs are wide open, the pussy has a little bit of hair, but it wasn't wolfing. I grab her ass bring her body to the edge of the table. I grab my dick with the left-hand then I slowly stick it deep inside her pussy. That pussy was tight and juicy. I stroke, stroke and stroke using my hips to push all inches in her. Her back is straight up as she holds my waist.

Every stroke I deliver she'll moans.

"Mmmmm mmmmm mmmmm damnnn!"

It gets to the point that she was too loud. Every stroke the volume turns up.
I stop in the middle of dicking her down. "Babe, you're loud as fuck."

"I can't help, it!"

"Alright, come here! I want to fuck you against the window."

She bends over putting her hand on the glass facing the city lights.
I grab her shoulder from behind and arch her back, then I stick my dick inside, spreading her walls open.

Her pussy is so wet that my knuckles got wet. Pushing my dick in her I'm beating the pussy up. In and out, in and out at a steady pace.

"Mmmmm mmmmm just like that," She moans.

I'm stroking her body fuckin her all crazy. As I tap that pussy her fingers are going down the window smearing the glass. I let go of her shoulder, with both hands, I spread her ass cheeks apart and I'm penetrating at the same pace. In and out I'm stroking, she's moaning with her mouth wide open.

"Oh I'm bout to cum, I'm bout to cum!"

My curled dick is hitting triggering her g-spot, got her about to bust like a fully loaded gun. I don't stop hitting that spot cause if so she'll lose that nut like keys in the couch. I keep my mind focused and my dick focused on making her cum.

"I want you to cum all on this dick, cum all on it!"

In no time, she screams announcing she's there. "Ohh, I'm cumming!"

I push my dick in her holding in as I quickly grab her mouth with my right hand to shut her up.

I don't get to nut but it cool that she came. There's about two minutes left of her break. Seconds after she leaves someone knocks at the door, then slowly opens it.

007. STRANGERS AGAIN

"Thank God it's Friday," I thought as I spit the toothpaste bubbles into the sink as the water in the faucet spiraled down the drain.

Knock! knock!

"Babe," Tia questioned pushing the door open and peeking in. I smiled staring her chocolate body down as she walked in. She was 5'2" with a nice set of 32C breasts and an ass that surprised me once she took her pants off. She had on a red scarf covering her long black hair and her face is just fucking gorgeous. Last night, I gave her a good dose of this Nyquil dick to put her to sleep.

"Damn! you're just going push the door open I didn't even say come in. How you gonna knock then bust open the door?"

She ignored my teasing and stepped in the bathroom then squatted down on the toilet. I heard the pee rushing into the toilet water. "Well, you didn't answer quick enough."

"What happened to you sayin' we wasn't that

couple?" I questioned after spitting out the toothpaste.

"What are you referring to?" Tia stared at me in confusion.

"I notice you don't give a fuck anymore, you just come in here then start pissing. I even caught you with the door wide open while you were taking a deuce. I almost died the other day." I continued my teasing and she rolled her eyes.

"Shut up silly, you're still here so I guess it didn't stink that much." She laughed.

"It's too early for this shit but you said it. I'm cool with shitting in front of you. I really don't give a fuck who's here."

"Why are we still talking about this?" She huffed before smiling at me in confusion.

"Because people like you busting down doors." I chuckled before heading out to the bedroom.

"I can walk in if I want. I pay half of the bills in this house!" She spoke matter of factly with a little aggression in her tone.

"I'm just playing big head, look at you getting all sensitive."

She walked in the bedroom seconds later following me. Here I was trying to avoid an argument and she continued our back and forth. "I'm not getting sensitive." Her bottom lip poked out like a spoiled 7-year-old little girl.

"Yeah, okay, look at your face you're pouting. Smile I still love you." I got behind her to wrap my arms around her body and kissed the side of her neck as we stood in front of the full-length mirror. I could tell she was still upset because she didn't return the love.

"Oh, you're not going say it back? look at us!" I said as I stared in the mirror at our reflection. She blankly glanced in the mirror. "We look good together huh? I want this for a lifetime." I kissed her neck some more and I continued teasing her. "You know you want to smile."

She had a serious grin on her face the cheekbones on her beautiful face could not resist.

"Look, look you're about to smile right now, here it goes, here it goes!" I said with goofiness in my voice.   She gave me a big smile as she put her hand over her mouth to cover her face.

"Ugh I hate you." she chuckled mad at herself for not being able to stay angry with me for long.

"I know you do." I smirked as I turned her around to face me. I grabbed her by the throat and kissed her soft lips.   Our lips touched, and then our tongues got tangled like shoelaces. As our tongues got knotted, she reached down in my grey boxer briefs and grabbed hold of my black, long, thick, eight-inch dick. She grabbed it like a hot iron and with a very slow pace, she stroked it.

"Can I get some before you leave? "

I glanced at the alarm clock on the nightstand on the left of the bed where I slept. I usually left at 7:15 am to make it to work at 8 am. Getting this started at 6:56 was a gamble but my clothes were already ironed and a quickie before a long day at work was welcomed. Sex was ten times better than a Red Bull or a Starbucks Coffee.

"Bend over." I said glancing at the bed to the right of us. She leaned forward, I kneeled down to my knees and spread her ass apart for a perfect passage to get a full wet lick of her pussy with every inch of my tongue. I wrapped my lips around her clit and slid my tongue gently across her pussy like a paintbrush.

"Oh shit! oh shit!" she wailed. I consistently slid my tongue across back and forth. I felt her legs quiver and heard her moans get louder and louder. I grabbed her ass with both hands and smushed her pussy into my face while I maintain focus sucking and licking on her clit. The pussy was a wet mess. I definitely had her juices flowing.

"I want that dick inside me," she said breathlessly.

Instantly, I stood to my feet with fluid dripping off my goatee, I grabbed hold of my dick and guided it to split the lips of her precious pussy; she was so fucking wet my knuckles even got messy as I made my entrance. Slowly I pushed every inch down inside then began to stroke.

"Oh my God!" she wailed   I reached for her

left shoulder and tightly grasped her neck then forcefully pulled her body into mine as I threw my dick inside her.

"Damn that pussy wet," I said while biting my bottom lip and penetrating at the same time.

"Yes daddy, yessss daddy!" she wailed grabbing a fist full of sheets.

"Cum on this! Dick cum on this dick!" I demanded as I continued to throw my waist against her ass and dig deep.

"Yes, oh yes daddy right there, right there! I'm going to cum on that dick!" she yelled.

Minutes later I felt her legs shaking.   "I'm cumming, I'm cumming!" she said. I kept on beating that pussy up from the back as I squeezed her throat tighter. "Oh shit, oh shit here I cum!" she announced as I felt her body get stiff like a stack of money. I pushed my dick far in her so she could savor the moment.   She flopped forward on the bed and I continued stroking at a slow pace; dipping my dick in and out her wet pussy.

"You gonna make me nut all in you." I said as I watch my dick slide in and out her pussy.

"Cum in me daddy, cum for me daddy" she said.

"OH DAMN, OH DAMMMNNNN!" I moaned as I felt a load of cum erupt out of my dick   "Damn babe here it cum." I felt a wave a chills come from my toes to the hair on my neck as I filled her insides like I was attempting to create a baby.

"Yess yes I feel it! Oh my Gosh I'm cumming again" she gripped the sheets tighter as her body got stiff like a statue. I held my dick in her while my heartbeat hurriedly as I tried to catch my breath.

"What the fuck babe, that dick is good." I smiled as she complimented my dick skills.

"Shit, Thank God you're on birth control because that was a boy that I just bust inside of you."

I gradually pulled my dick out of her pussy and slowly cum dripped down her inner thighs. I glanced at the time on the nightstand on the left side of the bed under the lamp next to an empty glass cup that I finished after the sex last night. The time read 7:32 am.

"Fuck," I said as the clock was striking 7:33. I stormed out the bedroom.

"I'll get you a rag." I got a green rag that was next to my white rag from behind the door

"Is the green one yours babe?" I said.

"Yeah the one behind the door."

The hot water from the faucet soaked the rag. I compressed it with a tight twist to force the water out. I went back in the room with the warm rag in hand and wiped her pussy clean.

"Damn baby that dick is so good, I wish you didn't have to work today so I can just fuck you all day and cuddle." She said as I wiped the cum from her thighs.

"Shit, I wish I didn't have to too." I paused. "Babe I might hang with the boys tonight." I said as I made my way back in the bathroom to hang the washcloth up on the shower rod

"That's fine I was going to the Krobar later on with Shanay and Lisa."

"Them hoes?" I sarcastically said as I buttoned up my shirt.   Shanay was hella sneaky. Last summer she stayed with us for a couple days after somebody robbed her apartment clean. She was terrified of going back to her place until she got an alarm system and cameras installed. It was only supposed to take two days. One Saturday I was off and Tia was at work Shanay showed plenty of sexual hints that she wanted to fuck me. She knocked on the bedroom door while I was comfortable lying in the bed watching ESPN Sports Center. She opened the door and had a peeled banana in her hand. Before she asked me if I wanted breakfast, she deep throated the banana slowly then she bit into it. On top of that she had on workout shorts and a sports bra; knowing damn well she's not a member to nobody's gym. Even though her body was built all in the right places with her brown tall legs, flat stomach and very attractive face I must say, lord know it's wrong if I even have thoughts of fucking this woman. I answered her question "Yes, I would love breakfast." As soon as she shut the door I plugged my charger into my iPhone 7 then grabbed the lotion and watched Pornhub on my phone to prevent myself from temptation. Shanay would mention that I'm a cutie and Tia is fortunate to have me as her man.

"Why it got to be them hoes?" she sighed expecting a sly comment.

"I don't know I just don't trust your one friend."

"Which one?" she quickly raised her brow.

"Shanay…"

"Why?" Now she was determined to get an answer and I was kind of regretting bringing it up.

"No reason." I said hoping to end the conversation. I never mentioned Shanay banana swallowing behavior but I always found myself staring at her lips at times wondering what that mouth do.

"So, where y'all going tonight?" Tia watched as I slid my feet into my socks.

" I think we're going to Krobar as well. I wasn't

going say nothing" I pushed my feet into my Loafers.

"Why not?"

"I don't know; I was just going to pop up on you."

"And that's when I would've acted like I don't know you."

The time read 7:54. ***"There's no way I'll make work on time."*** I thought to myself slowly down realizing I was already late.

"Well let's just act like we don't know each other then. If you're going to act like that."

"Look at you, you're in your feelings now" she smirked.

"Nah for real, let's play a game." I smiled getting an idea.

"What type of game?" She said as she pulled the sheets over her body, glancing directly towards me.

"How about we act like complete strangers?

176

You can get numbers and interact with other men and I can do the same with women. It's kind of like role-playing by the end of the night I'll spit my game to you and try to get you to come home with me. And who ever get the most numbers pays for dinner tomorrow."

"If we gonna play this game we're going to need rules because these bitches be thirsty."

"Okay, what's the rules?"

"First, no kissing or hugging up on no bitches. Two, no ex's or bitches you've already fucked in the past." I nodded listening to her boundaries.

"Okay, same for you." I agreed.

"Oh, you better not give your number to no one, save their number."

"Okay, we can save their number and put the skeleton face emoji next to the name. That will be proof of the numbers we got. And you're not allowed to interrupt when I'm interacting with someone."

"What else?"   The time was 7:59 am I was

fully dressed combing my nappy head and stuffing my wallet in my back pocket.

"Oh, one more thing before I go, no attitudes when the game is over. Let's just have fun."

***

I was sharp as a mothafucka. I stopped at the mall after work and bought new shoes and a fit to drip style in for tonight. When I came in with bags earlier Tia was eyeing me down with the swole face. She was also in her bag as well; she was absolutely pleasing to the eyes. Her appearance had me second-guessing the game. I'm literally throwing her to these thirsty ass wolves. She had a skin tight, short black dress on that was showing her smooth legs and her ass was plump and jiggly like Jello. Her hair flowed as the ceiling fan spun. Her makeup was on point blending well with her beautiful skin; Her brown eyes were framed by long lashes. She knew she was looking stunning because her nose was up, and attitude was very snooty towards me. She was definitely in game mode and it was only 10 pm.

While she took full control of the bathroom, I

was sitting on the foot end of the bed fully dressed watching stories on Snapchat revising my thoughts regarding this game. The game sounded fun but I couldn't see no man in my woman's face. Tia walked past me to step towards the body mirror to take a glance at herself. My eyes shifted from the screen of my phone to her taking photos of herself.

"You look nice." I said staring her down.

"Thanks!" She said feeling herself as she took shots of herself.

"You're welcome." I laid my phone on the white sheets of our queen bed. "Nah, for real you might win tonight." I said giggling.

"Here take a picture of me. Lisa and Shanay are around the corner," she said handing me the phone.

"Are you ready?" I asked watching her pose for the picture. She placed her hands on her hips and bust a beautiful smile. I snapped the shot "Ow I like that one."

"Let me see." she quickly snatched the phone

off me.   "Here take another one." she handed me the phone again then posed. This time she smiled with her head tilted to the left. I took the shot and looked down at the picture.

"Mmmmm I like this one too." I heard music thumping outside causing the front windows of my bedroom to vibrate. Just as I hand the phone over a horn honked twice.

"Thank you" she said then stepped towards the window, she split the blinds with her fingers to open and took a glimpse outside. "They're here!" she burst with excitement.

My body felt heavy like I was going to gravitate through the bed and straight through the floor into the neighbor's apartment down stairs. I was skeptical on allowing niggas to approach my woman. Soon as she grabbed her Louis Vuitton clutch bag I voiced my doubts. "Are you sure you want to play this game?"

She stood in the doorway and stared at me like I was crazy since it was my idea. "YES!" She answered rolling her eyes in the time her phone rang.

She answered her phone. "Hello, here I come girl." She went in the living room and continued to speak "Let get us some niggas I'm single tonight girl." she said laughing.

I jumped off the bed like I had hydraulics under my ass and I stepped hard into the living room. "NO THE FUCK YOU'RE NOT!" I roared

She laughed as she stepped towards the door to exit. "Are you big mad or little mad?" She calmly asked me before she continued her conversation on the phone.

"YOU'RE OVER HERE SAYING YOU'RE SINGLE!"

"Ow let me get out of here this nigga is big mad." she teased with laughter and shut the door.

She was right I was BIG MAD I couldn't believe I was sending her out with the wolves but let the games begin.

I drove by myself. My boys Lil Twone and Teddy were already inside the club. They came early to avoid the long line according to what Lil Towne cheap ass said. I really think they came to avoid the

$50 entry fee. It's was free of no charge to get in before 10 pm. The parking lot was packed with cars. I parked damn near a quarter of a mile from the club and when I finally got to the door, the lines were backed up to the moon. I could hear the music knocking from the outside and when the bouncer opened the door I seen flashing lights. The line was split into two. Ladies on the left fellas to the right. Strolling past the ladies line I could feel eyes sticking to me like gorilla glue.

"Hey Rowland." I heard a woman's voice. I glanced to the left smiling and waving as I kept my feet moving. Couple more steps I heard a soft raspy familiar voice scream my name I glimpsed to the left and there was Gina with the thick juicy big booty. She was overly excited. She seemed to want to jump out the line to hug me. She had a bright smile on her face with her eyebrows raised high. Gina was my ex-girlfriend who I dated my last year of college. She moved to Pittsburgh after graduating. We attempted to have a long distance relationship but that shit only lasted for four months even though Philadelphia was four and half hours away. Just imagine no sex for almost five months after having sex damn near every day. With open arms I hugged her tightly, she smelled pleasant like a fragrance of blossoms in the springtime and ice water.

"Gina butt! Hey how you been love?"

"I'm doing extremely well I'm just visiting the city for a couple days. How about you?" she said as she stood there with her friends.

"I'm coolin. I'm still in this damn city but I'm definitely good. you're still gorgeous." I said then I noticed Tia and Shanay in line a couple females in front of Gina. They were staring down my throat. My shoulders felt heavy like I was hauling a refrigerator on my back but I did not let them see me sweat. I wasn't feeling the game for a second and the fact that the woman I truly love is witnessing me interact with other women had me contemplating about reneging.

"Thanks. And you're still handsome" she said.   Then again I thought to myself this was my opportunity to make Tia jealous as I replayed the words she confidently spoke before she left the house *"I'm single tonight. Let's get some niggas."* Those words was fuel to my fire. I smiled while I held her hand and began to be flirtatious with Gina

"Thanks boo, if you spot me in here make sure you come see me, so I can get your pretty ass some drinks, okay." I said loud enough so Tia and friends could hear me clear as day.

"Okay" she said as she smiled. I walked pass Tia and her friends with a grin and shook my head realizing Tia didn't stand a chance. "Let the games begin." I mentally hyped myself up.

Tia seemed like she was flaming like a BIC lit on a cigarette tip and her friends were confused. They looked shocked as fuck.

After getting my manhood taken from the bouncer's strict body search, I was in this bitch, the club was lit as fuck. Lights flashed a variety of colors, the bottle girls walked around with bottles with sparklers in them going towards the VIP section, Dj Solo Dolo was on the ones and two's while the host Yalocal BigHomie screamed birthday wishes over the mic. The bar was completely crowded and so was the dance floor. Without a doubt my first stop was the bar. When I got to the bar everyone was shoulder to shoulder waving money at the two male bartenders, the guy next to me in all black with a neck full of gold chains and a mouth full of gold teeth was leaning on the bar.

"Yoooo me next, me next dawg come on!" He yelled aggressively. The bartender did not pay his ass any mind and served the female customer beside him. Waiting for another five minutes I eventually got my two cups of Hennessy and Coke with double shots of Henny. The beverages came to $15. I slid him a crisp 20-dollar bill then insisted he keep the change.

I linked with the homies Lil Twone and Teddy spotting them seated on the left end of the bar with damn near hundred empty plastic cups in front of them and a couple full drinks a Corona sitting on the bar.

"Y'all niggas ain't got on none of these shorties in here and y'all been here since the doors opened?" I teased, chuckling as my hand slapped against Teddy's hand. Teddy was a barber at Big Cuts barbershop in West Philly he was heavy weight, brown skin, fat boy with a full beard. He had lots of confidence and the women loved this fat fucker that's because he was always funny as shit. If you wanted your mood to be positive Teddy was the person you wanted to be around. The females called him Teddy but my name for him was Rick Ross or Tedd I swear this nigga resembled him.   I gave Lil Twone a high five following Tedd as Twone spoke.

"You the one with all the hoes," he said downing his beer.

"Nah, I be chillin for real."

Lil Twone was 5'9 dark skin, color of hot coffee on a Monday morning with long deadlocks, he had four-baby mama's and they were always sucking his pockets dry with child support. Last time we were together, he told me his baby mamas were getting $210 a piece. "Whatever yo, ever since you been eating Tia box you changed up on us. niggas only see you once in the blue moon." Lil Twone said.

"I'm 28 now I'm not trying to be all old chasing women, plus I ran through half of the shorties in here." I said as I sipped my drink.

"I thought your girl was coming with you?" Ted questioned a little puzzled to why I was alone.

"She's somewhere in here with Shanay and Lisaaaa." I dragged out my words as two beautiful ladies passed us. "Damnn," I thought out loud as my eyes turned into heart emojis. One was chocolatey and buttery with pure clear skin and nice full lips that were matted with black lipstick, her teeth were as perfect as it would be if you got new dentures but I'm sure her teeth were real. Her smile lit the club up, as dimples revealed the diamond piercings in both cheeks. Her hair was walnut brown with strands of highlights of blonde mixed in going straight down her back. My prediction...her breasts were approximately a 38D. She had a flat stomach, but she was thick in all the right places, filling in the short red off shoulder dress. A tattoo of butterflies appeared on her right shoulder and she also had leopard paw prints going up her thigh. Her ass had the appearance of being soft and the way the her backside jiggled as she walked. That ass was phat as fuck.

"I want the one in the black dress." Tedd called dibs damn near drooling on the bar table like a thirsty dog.

"Mee too" Twone agreed with Tedd in the act

of his of breaking his neck glancing back at the woman he admired.   The woman with the long sleeve black dress with the oval collar had light bright skin. She seemed to be mixed but I wasn't' sure. Her black hair was pulled back in a ponytail. She was not as thick as her friend but she was petite and short. She was super attractive, but the shape of her eyebrows turned me completely off. They were too damn thick as fraud as Miss Cleo future readings like she drew her brows on with a sharpie pen. Her brows made her seem extremely surprised the way they were arched high. If I was single I would still fuck but I would not glare in her eyes if I did dick her down because she'dl have the same surprised face when I was digging in the pussy and that would be awkward.

"Y'all can have her I think the chick with red dress looks better and I don't like shorty with the black dress eyebrows. I just want to lick my thumb and swipe her eyebrows" I said giggling   They both slightly laughed as well.

"You just like your women dark." Twone announced my biased.

"Damn skippy!" I sipped my drink as I caught

Tedd further staring at the ladies. "What you gonna do? Are you going speak to one of them?" I asked.

"No no, not by myself if one of you follow up and distract her friend." Tedd looked around for a wingman.

"Go ahead Twone be his sidekick," I volunteered him.

Twone's eye got as wide as a Powerpuff girl.   "No I'm cool you can tho." he said acting like a full-blown chicken.

In my peripheral, I caught a glimpse of Tia and her friends standing on the other side of the bar with two guys. The guy standing to the left beside my woman was tall. He had to be 6'5. He was a dark skin brother with gold chains shining with diamonds around his neck on top of his white V-neck t-shirt. He was bald headed with a full beard, both arms were covered with tattoos and both of his wrists and fingers were dripping in gold. Dude looked like a ball player for somebody's team.

"You know what I'll come with you," I said as

my eyes darted across the bar towards the homies.

It felt like every noise in the club went silent. Tia was smiling extremely too fucking hard like her jaw and cheekbones should hurt, she seemed extraordinarily happy. The two guys and her friend were laughing too, Lisa had her hand over mouth as the bartender served them.

What the fuck is so damn amusing? I just wanted to storm over there and grab her by the arm with force but "it's *only a game*" I reminded myself as Tedd interrupted my thinking.

"If you're down I'll definitely swerve on ol' girl. I just need you to distract the friend for me."

"Alright cool, let's take a shot first." I pulled out two 20-dollar bills and sat it on the bar. I glanced back across the bar and Tia had her phone out smiling while the bald headed, giant fucker whispered in her ear. My palms began to sweat and my mind was at a thousand with thoughts. Her glaring eyes looked at him the way she looked at me. *What could he be saying to my woman?* Then deeper thoughts kick in, *what if he takes my woman or what if she leaves with*

this man and rides his dick with that goddess, wet
pussy that I've been loyal to for the past two
years?   Tedd knew the bartender so he came in
seconds after he waved his hand to get his attention.

"YO ROWLAND!" Tedd screamed I snapped
out my deep thoughts

"What's up?" When I noticed the bartender
was taking orders I continued. "Oh, can I get a triple
shot of Hennessy and whatever they want." I needed
to drown my thoughts and play the game that I
invented because I was looking weaker than newborn
baby's arm.

"I pulled another 20 dollar bill out because a
triple shot will be at least close to $30 maybe $9 per
shot and whatever they wanted so I was looking at an
easy $50 plus a tip. They both got a shot of Apple
crown royal and Twone's broke ass wanted a Corona
for a chaser.   Soon as we down the shots my fucks
were missing and I was anticipating on playing the
game.

"So what's the plan Tedd?" I said as I eyed the
girl in the red dress then eyed my girl who continued

to smile while dude waved cash at the bartender.

"There's no plans, I'm just going to go over there and talk to her, you just come a second after."

"That sounds like a plan to me." I smiled amused by him needing a wingman. The ladies were standing in the corner to the right of us with their backs facing the wall, they were sipping on beverages in plastic cups, grooving to the tunes the DJ was playing. Tedd slowly stepped away from the bar then walked toward the ladies with confidence in his steps and shoulders relaxed. Twone busted out laughing.

"Who the fuck this nigga think he is Goldie?" Then he sipped his cold Corona that had water beads streaming down the cold bottle with a lemon floating inside. Goldie was a character from the 70's movie called The Mack. A flick about a Pimp coming up making hundreds and thousands dollars by selling women in the streets.

"At least he has heart unlike you. Niggas never believe you're getting pussy stories" I spoke shaking my head. Twone was known for lying on his dick so I only believed half of what he said. I downed the other half of the shot. As soon as I witnessed Tedd speaking to the ladies, I glanced across the bar and noticed Tia, her friends and the two guys were gone.

"Fuck it," I thought to myself then I trailed after Tedd's steps towards the ladies.

Soon as I made my appearance, Tedd introduced me. "This is boy my Rowland and this is Amber."

I extended my arms towards the woman with the black dress and shook her buttery soft hand. "How you doing?" I smiled at her staring her down before continuing. "And who is this beautif..."

Amber interrupted me before I can finish the sentence. "This is my cousin Stacy." Stacy extended her hand as I extended mine her hand was softer than cookies dipped in milk. I noticed her fingernails were a vivid red, which played well with the rose red dress she was wearing, her eyebrows were perfectly arched and appeared natural.

"How you doing Pretty? nice to meet you." I said as I glanced directly in her wildly appealing brown eyes.

"I'm doing fine, isn't your name @Mrhairpuller on Instagram?" She smirked before wrapping her lips around the straw in her glass.

"Oh yeah, that's me."

Her eyebrows rose and in the time, she rolled her eyes. "Don't you have a girlfriend; I don't break up happy homes?"

"Yea yea yea I I do" I stuttered glancing around the bar losing eye contact with Stacy. I wasn't going tell her no even if it was a game tonight.

"Would she be fine with you standing here trying to talk to me?"

I scratched the back of my head and smiled.   "Well I'm actually over here to be the wingman for my homie, I had no intentions on attempting to get your number." I lied.

"Oh okay!" she said jerking her neck back feeling stupid.

When Tedd got Amber's number, I shook Stacy hand again. "Nice meeting you."

An hour later, I had at least four numbers and attempted to get four more. I set my quota to eight. By 12:45am I was midway tipsy I went to all corners of the club and the ladies were showing me all kinds of love. They were giving me hugs, kisses, and smiles whiles the fellas were giving me high fives and handshakes.

I knew everyone considering that my mom moved from neighborhood to neighborhood when I was young. I went to a different school each year it seemed. When I got back to the bar where the homie damn near camped out, they were gorilla glued to the same seats they were in when I spotted them an hour earlier.

"I just got Tasha's number, I'm geeked for real." I gloated with a delightful smile on my face.

"You're still not going to fuck!" Twone blurted out confused at the point of our game.

"She asked for my number, she low key

approached me bruh."

"Like I said you're not going to fuck. She's so stuck on Cliff." I ignored Twone's hating and stared at Tia standing next to the VIP booth with her friend's. Since it was late, I felt it was time for me to go spit this panty dropping game to her. "Whatever nigga!" I waved him off before heading towards the VIP.

For a strange reason I was slightly nervous. it seemed like the lights went out in the entire club and a spotlight was shining from heaven gleamed on her as she stood there innocent like the pulchritudinous queen she was. The closer I got, I felt my heart throwing Mike Tyson, Holyfield, and Mayweather punches all in one force together through my chest, the people seemed to disappear as if it was just us.

"My name is Rowland I been peeping you the whole night. I find you very attractive."

Tia's eyebrows rose like the sun in the morning. "Oh, is that right"

"Yeah, so I had to say something before the night's over."

Shanay and Lisa were tuned in on our conversation like they were watching a drama scene on Love and Hip Hop: Atlanta.

"Well I guess you found every woman attractive tonight, I seen you in every bitches face."

I was at loss for words that she was making this harder than I assumed it would be. "I mean I was just..."

"Being a hoe?" She interrupted and finished my sentence.

"Being a hoe?" I repeated here words confused.

"I don't even know why your ass is over here in my space!"

My shoulders escalated and sweat bubbled while embarrassment flooded my poor little soul as she shut me down like a high school bomb threat. As the man I am, I pointed out the shit I witnessed.

"Well, I guess you're going home with the bald-headed nigga who was in your face all night?" I said with agitation and animosity in my tone.

"I guess" she shrugged her shoulders.

My eyes went low as my grin tightened on my face. I was flaming hot. "Oh yeah? alright you got it." I stepped back nodding my head then turned around to head back to the bar. The walk of happiness turned into the walk of shame. The environment instantly adjusted to reality. The stroll through the crowded club was not smooth. I had to squeeze through people and I even got bumped by accident by a couple drunks dancing. The lights were flashing, and the music seemed louder. After the shutdown I was equipped to go. My pride had been stomped on and thrown in the trash by the woman I loved.

"Stupid bitch." I thought as I stepped to the bar on the opposite side where my boys were. I didn't want to be bothered with them niggas either. As soon as got the bartender's attention I felt a woman's touch on my shoulder. I glanced over to the left and smiled at my college girlfriend Gina.

"I'm still holding you to that drink you promised me."

"I got you." I spoke remembering the promise I

made to her. Then I continued to order. "Um I want Hennessy and Coke and whatever this beautiful woman wants."

She put her elbows on the bar and leaned towards the bartender. "Can I have a Long Island ice tea?" The bartender scrambled as soon as the orders were taken. "So, let's catch up. How you been handsome?" she said smiling and biting her glossy bottom lip.

"I been maintaining that's about it. Same shit working and taking care of my son."

"That will be $15.50." The bartender sat the drinks on the bar.

I pulled the knot of cash out and gave him a 20-dollar bill "Thanks bruh I appreciate your service tonight keep the change."

He extended his arms to reach for the cash with a smile on his face. "Thanks man."

"No problem homie!" I nodded to him before bringing my attention back to Gina beside me.

"That's good, what else other than the adult life?" she picked up the conversation where we left it.

"I don't know, now days adulting is the only thing to do other than travel."

"You're right."

"What about you?" I asked sipping my drink.

"I'm just living. I have a nice place on the east side of Pittsburgh I'm loving it there. Even though there's no place like Philadelphia." She smiled putting her drink down and staring me down.

"I might have to ride up there someday. "

She took another swig of her Long Island Iced Tea and switched the conversation completely. "You know I haven't had an orgasm since I fucked you in college?"

That was over five years! *She had to be lying*, I thought to myself but I decided to play along. "Oh yeah, why not?" I asked licking my lips. "No man ate my pussy and filled my pussy up with a good stroke game like you. There's nights I watch our video we recorded and masturbate to it"

My eyebrows raised with shock and I laughed not knowing how else to react. "Damn you still have that shit? That was damn near six years ago on your last night living in Philly."

Her eyes shifted downward with embarrassment. I think she thought I was going to be judgmental but that wasn't the case. She had my full attention now. "Let's cut to the chase I want to fuck you."

My jaw could've dropped to my ugly toes that I kept covered with socks. "You want to fuck me?" I asked to confirm what I was hearing.

"Yes, let's leave now!"

My mind was racing like horses up for bets. I was ready to take this deal because her pussy was A1 back in college. We used to fuck all day and all night between classes and studying for exams. I heard lots of commotion behind me as I contemplated this proposal.

I glanced back, and spotted Tia getting held back from her friends as a guy was screaming from the top of his lungs. In seconds, he titled his cup and threw a drink directly in her face.   The conversation quickly ended with Gina. I removed myself from the bar with fire in my steps. With my forearm, I pushed people out the way and quickly stepped to this short stocky light skin nigga with his arm ripping through his True Religion Shirt. I didn't notice what else he was wearing because in seconds he was wearing my fist across his fucking face. I swung on this nigga punching him so damn hard he would have thought I threw a red brick at his face.

"BITCH ASS NIGGA!" I shouted as my fist connected with his face. People in the crowd shouted "ohh," "ahh," and even an "oh shit," was heard in the crowd. Dude fell straight to the floor as Tia's friends released her. She ran directly towards me with open arms to hug me tight. I didn't even mind that she had alcohol dripping from her hair as she was soaked in alcohol.

"Let's get out of here." I said right as the security rushed through the crowd pushing people out the way to get to the scene. I noticed the bald head guy standing there with fear in his eyes.

Bitch ass nigga, why didn't his bitch ass do anything? I thought to myself. People had their phones out recording. I wouldn't be surprised if this shit went viral tomorrow because I punched this nigga so fucking hard my hand was swollen like a mothafucka. We didn't have a chance to escape. The oversized bouncers got to us and damn near carried us out the club. When we got in my 2016 black Chevy Impala she reached in the glove compartment for napkins to clean herself.

"Sorry I was mad because I was jealous that you were talking to all them girls." She apologized before I could even pull out the parking lot.

"At first, I wasn't going play until I seen you all in that bald head niggas face, I thought you don't like bald niggas."

"Who Ace?" She laughed as I stopped at the first red light and flicked the right turn signal. "That's Shanay cousin. He was in my face and he's not my type whatsoever. His breath smells like mothballs I would never in a thousand years."

"I'm just saying that's not what it looked like."

"I was playing his ass. Every nigga that came my way got curved as well. I wasn't playing that stupid game." she admitted.

"I see you even curved me."   Green lights. Green lights. I flew past a few yellow ones too to avoid the red lights. By the time, we got in front of our home the conversation changed drastically. "Swear to God I love you and I don't want no other woman!" I spoke genuine words as I stared at her in the passenger seat.

"I know," she said with firm conviction in her voice.

I turned the key to turn off the vehicle then pulled the key out. "Come here."

She leaned towards me with her left elbow on the armrest.

"Babe I love you." I said with certainty feeling bad that I was the only one playing our little game tonight. "I just," I started and she quickly interrupted me with a kiss.

Under the orange streetlights and the dashboard glowing, our lips touched with passion then our tongues tied and slid against each other. Her kisses were soft and warm. I grabbed the back of her head for deeper kisses and sparks went through my body. Calmly, raindrops tapped the windshield. Seconds later the rain came down like cats and dogs, our tongues untied and lips disconnected.

"Let's go in the house." she suggested.   The rain sounded like it wanted to break through the roof.

"Alright, on the count of three."   A car road past with bright headlights damn near blinding us as I gave instructions. "Ready 1.2.3" I unlocked the doors.   We both swung the doors open and slammed the doors shut, running to the porch attempting to dodge the raindrops.   In the time I unlocked the front door we both were soaked and breathing heavily. Tia's hair was flat with water dripping from the tips down to her face and my shirt was stuck to my back revealing my cut arms and chest.

"Oh my God it's raining hard, did you lock the doors?"

I turned the doorknob on the front door and slightly pushed to open then I pressed the remote hanging on the keychain to lock the car doors. "I'm about to now."

Just as Tia stepped foot in the house first, lightening flashed following by a blustering boom. When I stepped in following her I closed the door behind me. Right as she kneeled to remove her heels I extended my arm to reach for her throat.

"No keep those shoes on." I demanded with mischief in my voice. I felt her breathing get heavy in my palm as she swallowed her saliva. I glanced in her eyes then I inserted my thick long tongue down her throat. Our tongues slapped against each other as she moaned with ecstasy. I detached my mouth from her mouth after seconds of tongue dancing. I forcibly pushed her backwards against the plush stairway rug that led upstairs to the bedroom. I released my hand from her throat. She knew I was not toying around by the genuine stare she presented to me. Deep down inside I think my controlling act was making her pussy flutter as her juices rushed down in anticipation of what was next. *"She wants this dick,"* I thought to myself as I rapidly kneeled to my knees as she sat helpless on the fourth step. Aggressively I pushed her dress up to her stomach, snatched her nude colored thong from her waist and pulled them from under her pumps. She bit her bottom lip as I slid her legs apart. I planted deep kisses on her left thighs leaving a trail of my full lips.   She moaned glancing into my eyes as she tried her hardest not to shut them, I licked her clit with every dripping inch of my tongue to send a spark through her body

"Oh, my God" she wailed. Then I switched and kissed her right thigh. Teasing would guide her to the first orgasm. After minutes of caressing her lower body I wrapped my lips around her throbbing clit and built lots of saliva inside my mouth even though her pussy was already running like a faucet from me previously teasing her private parts. I slid the tip of my tongue horizontal across the clit back and forth at a steady mild pace to stimulate her sensitive nerve.

"Mmmmmmmh" she moaned as her body rose like raw biscuit dough inside a hot oven. When it's all said and done I would be the man buttering her insides.   While I slid my tongue against her delicious clit, my lips were moving like I was chewing gum with my mouth closed to massage the outer of her pussy. Her juices ran through the corner of my lips rolling down my goatee and dripped down the crack of her ass. Her moans grew as I began to speed the pace of the strokes of my tongue beating her clit while her heels dropped, tumbling down two steps onto the floor.

"Yes baby! yes baby!" Her screams echoed bouncing off the walls in the lobby of our duplex apartment. Her legs were stiffer than the Statue of Liberty and she was breathing massively as I sent an electric shock of pleasure throughout her body to her palpitating heart while I triggered her clit.

"I'm cummin daddy!"

I continued to lick and stimulate her sweet tasty clit. I began to hum to give vibration to her pussy so the orgasm would be explosive.

"I'm cummin, I'm cumin!" Moans came out her mouth.

My eyes closed tightly concentrating as I worked my jaw to give her my everything.   Her moans spontaneously stopped and her body squirming came to a pause. The room got quiet and the only noise heard was the wet squishing sound of my tongue sliding against her pussy. Her soul lifted and body melted like candle wax on a night without electricity. She burst out howling as she gripped the back of my head with the strength of a beast.

"Fucck" her words stretched with pleasure leaking out her mouth.   I released my face from between her thighs, her legs loosened. I immediately withdraw her dress from over her head and then I reached around the back and snapped her bra off with a simple snap of a finger.

Her body showed every sign of weakness like I sucked the life out of it. She laid there disabled like she had not one bone to hold her flesh as she quivered from the aftershock.   I kicked my shoes off and got undressed in a flash, my dick was standing at salute, black, hard, and strong. She snapped to reality as soon as she witnessed what was in front of her that she dearly loved and admired. She leaned toward me as she remained seated on the steps, stretching her left arm to grab the base of my thick dick, she slowly beat my gorgeous piece of meat that had healthy veins bulging out and was hard as a metal pole. She brought the dick near her lips then she licked around the cone and stroked at the same time. Chills ran through my spine like someone had dumped ice water on my back with a Gatorade Beverage Cooler like coach winning a championship game.

"My dick, is this mines baby." she assured as our eyes connected like WIFI."

"Yes, it's yours all yours..." My eyes were forced closed as she took the dick deep in her mouth. My balls tapped her chin as she took me in and out, saliva cascaded her chin at the same time tears formed in her eyes. She let her head back and a string of saliva bridged from the tip of my dick to her lips. Tia's mouthpiece was drastically a wet mess. She stuck her tongue out as she grasped the center of my dick then slapped it against her mouth mouth while she glanced at me with delight in her eyes and smirk on her face. She was enjoying the fact that I was pleased.

I yanked her right arm and spin her body around at full tilt. "Bend over" I instructed as I held a fist full of her hair in my right hand. She put both knees on the third step and with the free hand, I guided my dick to split the lips of her dripping wet precious pussy. Slowly I pushed every inch in balls deep, filling her walls with my blessings as I pushed her back down with the hand I released from my dick to give an arch in the spine. Her breath escaped from her soul then returned as I pulled back to the head of my dick remaining between her lips. Then again, I push the dick deep in her so far she felt that shit poke her heart.

"Mmmh damn baby," she breathlessly wailed.

I pulled her hair back with aggression then leaned towards her and whispered with animosity in my words "This is my fucking pussy." I began to stroke at a mild pace thrusting far in her.

"Yea daddy it's yours, it's yours," she mentioned to each and every individual stroke.

"I love you daddy, I love you," she's screamed with a crack in her voice.

"You love me, throw that shit back," I demanded with sternness.

Her hands were already placed on the step to support the hard strokes I was sending so she turned around and used that as leverage to push herself back at the dick.

"Yes, just like that Mmmh just like that Tia," I complimented her motivating her to maintain the motion. It was teamwork the way she met my strokes throwing it back. I went in and out the pussy beating up the center like a snare drum, moans, and curse words uttered out both of our mouths as we fucked each other like there was no tomorrow.

"Oh yes, yes baby here I cum," she announced.   I glance down and watched my shiny dick pound her backside. "Here I cum baby" she made certain I heard.

"Cum on this dick, come on this dick" I begged for her to climax on my wood. I stroked her nonstop with a passion; I grasped her by the throat to pull her back against my chest then repeated myself in a low mutter.

"Cum on this fucking dick."   In seconds as I was applying pressure to her throat Tia's body weakened as she unraveled, cumming hard on my dick.

"Fuccccccccck daddy," she screamed while I held it inside as we both breathe heavily, chest sinking in and out in the time our bodies sweat against one another.

I plopped down on the second step with my dick standing strong, with her back facing my front she gradually sat decreasing herself down my pole full of her ejaculate fluids she relived on me. She had both hands clenched to my knees, raining down on this dick, leaving flood with her wetness. Five minutes into I felt myself about to burst, she slowed her speedy pace of bouncing and road the tip. "Shit shit shit keep going," I said as she moaned.   In a bat of an eye my dick erupted like a volcano squirting all inside her, filling up her pussy up with my babies.

***

Weeks later in a gas station a short white lady with wrinkled skin and a fucked up hair-do in the mid 30's, with a dingy white t-shirt with ketchup stains on it was standing in front of me debating on lottery scratch offs.

"Can I get 2 of those $5 lottery tickets, no 3 tickets?"   As the Indian cashier ripped the first ticket she changed her mind again. "Never mind I just want 2 tickets."

After she paid for the tickets, I decided to buy the third ticket she was hesitant to purchase.

"You know what I'll buy the ticket that lady didn't buy and can I get $45 on pump 2?"

The lady eyeballed me as spoke while she scratched her tickets at the lottery checker that was on the right wall.

"$50 even." the cashier gave me the total. I never bought a lottery ticket, but I received a dollar ticket from my job as a cheap ass Christmas gift, but I didn't win a damn prize. I scooted to the side where the second register was closed, I grabbed a pretty, shiny, copper penny out my pocket then scratched the four numbers at the top 4 34 56 69. *Reveal the*

matching numbers and win the prize under the numbers. There were four rows with four chances to win, the first three rows I scratched were nothing and on the fourth the number 69 shown

"Oh shit!" I screamed with excitement in my voice. The lady glanced at me with a snotty look on her face. I scratched under the number revealing my prize of five thousand dollars.

"Oh fuck I won 5 thousand dollars!" I began screaming. The lady tossed her tickets in the trash then stormed out the store with shame written all over her face. Weeks later the day I received the money, I spent $4000 at Jared's Jewelry on an engagement ring for Tia. The weekend after the purchase of the diamond ring, I reached out to both of our families and told everyone to meet me at the movies and get tickets for *The Wild Life* a kid's movie. We arrived late, so the lights would be completely out in the theater. When the credits were rolling at the bottom of the step I got on one knee.

"Tia Williams would you marry me?" I proposed glaring in her eyes. She stood there with her hand over her mouth astounded, tears formed in her beautiful eyes.

"Yes, I will Rowland," with a smile and watery eyes she answered.

Soon as she gave me acknowledgment both of our families applauded, she looked up and was overwhelmed with joy blended with tears of happiness rolling down her face when she caught a glimpse of our families.

...

My son just turned four, two months ago. He's a little chubby boy and funny as hell. He's brown skin with chunky high cheek bones, when he smiles his dimples make everyone melt. When I first laid my eyes on him I fell in love and named him after myself. After retrieving my son from his mother's house on a Friday evening, Baby Rowland sat in that back seat in his car seat while Tia sat in the passenger seat taking selfies on Snapchat with her engagement ring, she was still ecstatic from last week's proposal.

"Can we get candy daddy? I have money." Baby Rowland spoke. I glanced back and seen him waving his wrinkled dollar bill.

"Oh you got all the money, can I have some money little dude?" I joked He extended his arm attempting to give me his only dollar.

"Daddy here?"

"Nah, I'm cool son," I said smiling while sitting at a red light.   It's a gorgeous evening. It's in the mid 70's and everybody in their mother is outside enjoying this beautiful day, when we pulled up to the corner store in west Philly people were standing in front.

"Babe, do you want something from in here."

"Just a bottle of water."   I stepped out the vehicle then unbuckled my son's car seat in the passenger's rear; he hopped out with his tiny black and white Jordan shoes, fitted jeans and a white t-shirt with a big Jordan logo in the center. Stepping beside me the small version of myself, the feeling of being a father is beyond great, words can't express the love I have for my little man. There were two pretty black girls around the age of Jr with colorful beads in their hair slapping hands

"Patty cake, patty cake, baker's man. Bake me a cake fast as you can," they sang while waiting for a bus with their mother, there were a few others at the bus stop as well. A teenage light skin boy with nappy hair stepped out the door as I reach for the doorknob to open, he held the door.

"Thanks, brotha," I said to the young man.

"No problem." he replied   Baby Rowland wants just about every sweet tooth killer candy in the small store. BBQ lays chips, fruities, peach rings, fishes and a Huggie juice, which we call quarter waters he was snatching shit off the shelf as if everything was free. I grabbed Tia's water and chips for myself then bought a few lottery tickets

"I might get lucky again," I thought as I made my purchase.   When we stepped outside the little girls were still slapping hands singing.

"Patty cake patty cake,"   My son lifted his bag of chip up towards me.

"Daddy open please?" He asked for my assistance.   I stopped in the middle of my tracks and grabbed his

218

chips to open. As I pulled the chip bag open like a zip lock bag I heard tires digging deep into the pavement. "Remember Me?" words escaped from a man's mouth as shots fired; a flaming hot bullet went through my shoulder.   I leaped on top of my son as shots rang out ripping skin out my right thigh, arm, and neck. The only noise I heard was baby Rowland.

"Daddy" he screamed in a piercing cry   I open my eyes for a second and witness blood covered over my son white shirt then everything went blank. Daddy was the last words I heard.

...

"Daddy" I opened my eyes laying in the hospital bed with a tube connected to my body. Jr was sitting in the chair next to me with a Band-Aid on his elbow smiling holding the lottery ticket I bought. My Mother was on the foot end of the bed with tears forming as she witnessed my waking. Tia, my fiancé was standing next to me holding my right hand with tears running down her beautiful face onto the thick white sheets the hospital provided to me.

Later in the day on the 5 o'clock news, they stated the

police found the killer of the 6-year-old girl and two wounded. The guy who shot me and killed that young girl playing Patty Cake Patty Cake was that nigga I punched in the club a month ago.

008. STUCK

"Yo bro I won't be able to check out the building with you, Meme wants me to stay at the hospital with her but send me some flicks and videos."

Earl, my business partner, texted me letting me know in advance that he wouldn't be able to tour the building we were supposed to build a recording studio in. I needed him to be there especially going into this venture together, but if anybody understood that family came first it was me. Anxious to see what I was possibly stepping into I arrived at the site twenty minutes earlier than the expected time. I sat in my car and glanced through the paperwork in my briefcase while I waited for the realtor. For some reason my nerves were on edge while I organized my paperwork and made sure I had everything I needed.

Just as I was closing the briefcase, I peeped a red BMW pull up to the curb across the street from where I parked. The door swung open, and I couldn't help but be impressed by the long legged, chocolate complexion, long black hair, tight dress wearing real estate agent.

"Oh damn," I said quietly to myself as she continued to catch my eye like a baseball falling into an outfielder's glove. As much as I wanted to switch into player mode, I kept my cool, switched my focus back down onto my briefcase, and remained professional. I finished gathering all of my paperwork, stepped out of my car with my briefcase and a bottle of water, and made my way across the street to the doors of the gray metal building.

The agent was in the small dusty lobby standing in front of the elevator doors talking on the phone. Noticing she was on the phone I softly knocked on the opened door three times.

"Hold on," I heard her say in a soft tone putting whoever she was talking to on hold.

"Come in!" She yelled towards the doorway. "I'm gone call you right back girl I got a client coming in," I heard her speak into the phone as I walked

"Earl?" She questioned shaking my hand.

"No, I'm Lamar his business partner. Earl couldn't make it so it's just me today. How you doing?"

"Well Hello Lamar I'm Janet and I'm fine thank you, and yourself?" She spoke with such a warm confident smile on her face.

"I'm good, just trying to find a building so we can get the ball back rolling on finishing this cd."

"What are you interested in using the space for if you don't mind me asking?" She inquired genuinely curious.

"A recording studio. This is actually the third time we had to relocate because of neighbors' complaints about noise."

"Well this is your place." She spoke with a big smile and placing her arms out as if I had won the jackpot on a gameshow. "You can make all the noise you want in here! So shall we begin the tour?"

"Lead the way," I extended my hand out directing her to walk in front of me. As she headed towards the elevator, I couldn't help but watch her work that tight dress that hugged every curve on her body. I wanted her more with every step she took. I took a sip of my water to control my thirst and continued to

As she pressed the up button on the elevator she brought up Earl. "I hope things are okay with him, he seems like a nice guy."

"Yeah, he's definitely good peoples. We been producing and mixing songs together since high school. That's my homie" I smiled as the elevator door opened. We stepped in and as the door began to close she pressed 3 on the old worn number pad.

"Well I'd like to hear y'all work one day if you don't mind."

"No no, I don't mind actually I'd like that." I couldn't keep the smile off my face as I threw game.

The dim light over our heads flickered a couple times as the elevator went up. We both looked up at the lights concerned and as if she was reading my mind she brought it up before I could.

"I'll have the maintenance man put a new light bulb up tomorrow."

"Uh oh problems already?" I said jokingly just to see her flash another one of those beautiful smiles, "But on a serious note how are the people on the first two floors? I don't wanna invest time and money and then have to relocate again."

Just then the elevator stopped, and the door opened." There's a photographer who owns the facility on first floor, he's hardly here. you might see him once, maybe twice a year. The woman who owns the second floor died in a car accident two years ago, she was a famous painter. Her son comes here every year on her birthday but that's about it. Her family's not ready to let go so they keep the space, I promise you, you won't have any problems with this space, except maybe a flickering light bulb or two." She laughed stepping off the elevator.

Walking through the short hallway, I followed her to the small kitchen; there was a new black and silver stove next to a big silver refrigerator and plenty of cupboard space. Very impressed by the kitchen alone I continued to observe the space taking pictures while I moved along. I couldn't lie the lobby and the elevator definitely had me second-guessing this place. Janet gave me information about what was being done in the space while I observed.

"We just remodeled the entire kitchen; I had them knock the walls down to add more space and bought all new appliances."

I took a few more pictures while she continued to tell me about the large loft area, the bathroom, and the small bedroom.

"I'm feeling this." The more she spoke, the more she won me over. The room across the hall was perfect; there wasn't too much space or too little, just enough to build a booth and sitting space for the guests. Janet walked with me as I continued to observe the place. I tried to keep my focus on the details of the efficiency, but I found myself getting more and more distracted by the beautiful woman showing me the space.

"I bet if Earl was here he'd definitely say this is a go. Matter fact I'm texting him now."

"Okay," She laughed.

"Damn Never mind my phone about to die so I guess I'll make the decision on my own. So how much would it be to rent out this space? I could see myself making all kinds of music in here."

"It's very cheap, you're looking at 800 dollars a month plus utilities."

"Sounds good sounds good," I said licking my lips and looking Janet in the face. "Can we schedule another appointment within the next two days? If it was all up to me, I'll be scribbling my signature on every dotted line right now but me and Earl are in this together I guess." I chuckled, and she soon joined me amused by my tone.

"Okay, um how about Saturday at noon? Is that ok?"

"That's cool. Saturday I'll be free I'm sure Earl will be here with me after I tell him about this spot." We shook hands and began to make our way to the elevator. "So how long have you been a realtor? and how you get started?"

"It's been five years I've been in the business. It's actually a family business. It began with my mother she used to flip houses with my step dad. When he passed she showed me the ropes of buying and selling houses and I've been doing it ever since." She pressed the down button to bring the elevator to the floor.

"Oh, that's what's up, young successful black woman. I love to see that."
"Thank you," she said flashing a smile while the elevator opened.
"You're welcome" I replied watching her press the button to go to the first floor.
"So, what made you want to be a music engineer? My younger brother actually wants to be a rapper." she giggled "He's 13 though, at that age who doesn't want to be a rapper? I heard one of his..." Midsentence the elevator light went out and darkness surrounded the both of us.
"Oh damn, I hope we don't get stuck in here, it feels like were still on the third floor."
She pulled an iPhone out her purse shining the light on the numbers on she pushed the one button continually as if it was going to miraculously make us move.
"I hope not either," she said right as the elevator jerked hard.
"Oh shit," I yelled out nervously as Janet dropped her phone to the floor panicking and screaming.

"Oh my Goooood, oh my God!"
The elevator dropped again, during her screaming.
"Sit on the floor and hold the rail just in case the elevator cable snaps." In the inside I was nervous but on the outside, I was cool, calm, and collected not

wanting Janet see me sweat.

I put my briefcase on the floor and sat in the far-right corner of the elevator. Janet got a hold of her iPhone and sat in the left corner. She sat there with a deadly stare on her face making it easy to see she was terrified.

"I'm about to call my mother to see if she can have someone come out to fix this and get us out."

The lights came back on right as she tried to make a phone call, my hopes were up and I just knew the elevator was going to operate normally.

"Shit!!!! I don't get no service in here." Janet smacked her phone frustrated that she wasn't any closer to finding help.

"I got four percent of battery left; you can try to call her on my phone." I turned my phone on and stared over at her. "What's your mom's number?"
"It's 4 1 2 7 1 2 4 3 2 6..."

As she spoke, I dialed the number. "Did you say 4 3 2 6?" I pressed call then I slid the phone across the floor. "Here, you got to make it quick my phone about to tap out." As soon as she picked the phone up off the floor it died immediately.

"What the fuck? Your stupid phone died. What are we going to do?"

"I can try to push the doors apart." I stood in front of the elevator and placed my fingers in between the cracks. I used every muscle in my arm to open the door getting nowhere quickly. It opened about two inches and after trying for a few minutes, I got frustrated and let go. I removed my white button up shirt then tried again, attempting to spread the doors apart again. "You think the briefcase can fit? Push it between the crack."

"Okay," she said grabbing hold of the briefcase sounding as if she had nothing to lose.

The elevator door still wouldn't open more than two inches. After about 10 minutes of trying I had to give it up. My fingertips were in pain, my heart was racing, and I was sweating, at this point, I was convinced there was no way out. Frustrated I sat on the elevator floor thinking of my next move.

"There still no signal, this is crazy we're really stuck in the elevator." Janet groaned trying to use her phone again

"I know, crazy as hell. Where you from? If you don't mind me asking" I hoped conversation would ease her nerves.

"I'm from Monroeville."

"You up there with them rich white folks huh?"

"It's not what it's cracked up to be, there's a lot of black people out there too."

"So, you like the Gateway Gators huh?" I laughed, "Woodland Hills used to tap that ass back in the day."

"Yeah, right we use to tap their ass." She smiled rolling her eyes at me.

"What year you graduate?" It was now my turn to quiz her.

"2007 what about you?

"2006. So, you have any kids?"

She scooted over towards me with her phone in hand

to show me pictures. "Yeah, a boy he's three." She slid her finger across the phone screen and smiled, "and he's bad."

While scrolling she passed A picture of a man holding her son. "That must be your man or baby's daddy?" I kindly asked.

"Yeah, he's in jail now, he's doing 20 years in the Feds cause he just
couldn't leave them streets alone, I tried to change his ways but he did what he wanted."

"Damn, I tried to tell my young nigga, the streets don't love you, they just take you away from the people who do."

"I swear and that's what happened to us, I'm here to raise a little boy to be a man on my own." She sighed as the lights went out again almost unfazed by the elevator game.

"Them damn lights" I sat back against the wall a bit annoyed myself.

She laughed, "I know it's already bad enough were stuck in an elevator, so anyways what about you Do you have a wife, girlfriend or someone you care for?"

"I talk to a few girls right now but I'm single as fuck."
"Oh, okay playa playa. Do you have any little ones?"
"Yeah two boys, Chris and Chance."
"Are they by the same mother?"
"Yeah, both from the same woman."
"Oh, ok that's what's up. So basically, you can talk to who you want and fuck who you want huh?" She laughed.

"Haha! I guess you can say that. To be honest, I might be addicted to sex. I get pleasure out of pleasing a woman, I love women."

"You don't got to have multiple females to fulfill your need to please, you can have one woman who will give you your needs, and fuck you better or as good as all them girls."

"Yeah You right, what you trying to say though? Are you that one girl for me?"

"Boy, you trying to be fresh. I'm too much woman for you. You wouldn't know how to handle me mentally or physically."

"Don't doubt me, My finances might not be on your level but I am a man, and I'm well educated. I'm not going to boast on how I am when it come to being physical but I will have you coming back for seconds."

I was now intrigued taking her last words as a challenge.

She twisted her lips and sucked her teeth. "Is that right? Coming back for seconds huh?"

"I'm serious as hell, if I ate you right now I'll have you running up these walls." I smirked confident in myself.

"That sounds kind of kinky I'm stuck in the elevator with a stranger who's talking about eating my vajayjay, hmm I might have to think about this."

I licked my lips watching her give me the side-eye.

"What you thinking 'bout?" I teased. "Come here and I'll show you."

I scooted over to the same corner as her and within seconds, she pulled the hair on my chin to bring my lips towards her red lips and kissed me. Her lips were soft, wet, and tasted like strawberries. She gave me two pecks, we looked in one another's eyes then our tongues got involved. *It's always them pretty chicks who are the freakiest.* I thought to myself as our tongues tied like a knot. I kissed under her neck above her gold herringbone as she threw her head back against the wall and moaned.

"Mmmmmm Mmmmm," a moan escaped her lips as I aggressively pulled the dress up her thick thighs. I ducked below the waist and kissed on each thigh rubbing my tongue up and down sending chills down her spine. I caressed her body while I pushed the dress up some more revealing the fact that she wasn't wearing panties. Instantly turned on I placed my face between her inner thighs and sucked her clit with my wet mouth. She melted in seconds changing from a sitting position to lying flat on the floor. I cuffed her thighs and licked and sucked the pussy full throttle at a constant pace. She moaned loudly grabbing the back of my head pushing my face in her juicy vagina. I kept my tongue and lips moving breathing out of my nose as she pushed and pushed my head harder into her pussy humping my face at a furious rate. The lights flickered on and off like club strobe lights as she kicked her heels off giving herself better opportunity to push off the elevator floor and into my face. I pushed her feet back together towards her head then stuck my long tongue in her pussy fucking her pussy with it. I bounced my face in and out shaking my face against it. I could tell she was enjoying my actions due to her heavy breathing, extremely loud moaning, and her back lifting from the floor numerous times. I continued to suck and lick her like I was on the verge of dying of starvation and her moans made me go even harder. In no time her legs got stiff and her toes twisted up.

"Fuckkk I'm cumming." She yelled while banging her fist on the elevator wall hard as fuck and her back arched as the orgasm took over her body. I continued eating her at a furious rate while she released her nut pushing my forehead back removing my face from her tasty lady fruits.

"Oh my God," she moaned still laying on the floor In the same position. "You weren't lying about those skills of yours." She smiled staring at me in disbelief.

"Word, you like that huh?"

"Um huh," she said bringing herself to her knees, "Now stand up so I can taste that dick."

I couldn't stand up quick enough. I rose to my feet, placed my back against the wall, and unbuckled my pants dropping them to my shoes. I guess the floor was too hard to be on her knees because she bent down standing on her toes grabbing hold of my rock hard dick. I held onto the rails looking down at her while she swallowed my dick looking me straight in my eyes. The look in her eyes let me know she was about to suck the life out of my dick and I was ready for it. She spat on my dick to make it moist while she slowly beat my dick. She wrapped her mouth around

my dick and bobbed her head back and forth stroking at the same pace causing butterflies to rise in my stomach. Soon as I began to get really into this extreme act of kindness the elevator jerked causing her teeth to rub against the head of my dick feeling like a needle sliding across the tip. I quickly removed my penis grabbing hold of it and yelling out in pain "Ow ih ih ih." She glanced up towards me, with her hand over her mouth,
"Oh my gosh I'm sooooo sorry, the elevator shook bad my head just bobbed!"
        "It's cool babe, that shit just caught me off guard, I'm good though."
She grabbed hold of my dick again and kissed it gently,
"I'm sorry" she genuinely spoke kissing it a few more times.
I gently pulled her up by her wrist and stared in her eyes sensing her sincerity. "Stand up and take your dress off and bend over." I demanded bringing her from her knees to her feet. I reached in my pocket, grabbing out the Magnum that I always kept on hand. She turned around and giggled.

        "Oh, I guess you're always prepared huh? You def must be a ladies' man."
I laughed while removing the condom from the wrapper and rolling it down over my dick. "I told you I like women, now bend back over." I slid my penis inside of her thrusting it all the way in. I pushed her back down to arch her spine as I began to stroke her

233

from behind throwing every inch in her while pulling her body into mines.

Moaning loudly she gripped the metal rail, while I took in a fistful of her hair not giving a damn if it was weave or not. I twisted my wrist pulling her hair back while I used my other hand to arch her back. Thrusting in and out moving my hips to establish my stroke I fucked her at a steady pace while she moaned out.

"Ugh Fuck me! fuck this pussy harder harder owwww."

I pushed her face into the elevator wall and fucked her more aggressively; dicking her down something serious as she threw her ass back at me.

After a small session of giving back shots I picked her up off her feet and fucked her against the wall in the corner. I held her by the ass as she wrapped her arms around my neck. The lights went completely out in the elevator as our bodies banged on the wall. I couldn't hold her body up too long so my arms weakened after at least five minutes of holding her up so I put her down and positioned myself on the floor.

"Come ride this dick," I demanded and in no time, she stepped over top of my body and positioned herself right onto my dick sliding down it like a pole. I cuffed her ass as she bounced on my dick like a trampoline. I felt hands clawing my chest but I couldn't see her facial expressions because it was pitch black leaving me with her moans to tell me exactly how the dick was feeling. I bent my legs up fucking her back lifting my lower back and hips up

234

from the floor.

"Here I cum, here I cum," she moaned out as I continued to dig inside of her. "I'm cumming I'm cumming," she's continued yelling out stiffening up and slowing down her pace. I pushed my dick up in her and held both of her shoulders down to put more pressure into the nut.

After she released all over my dick she rode me slowly dipping her pussy on the tip of my penis and in no time, I felt an energy taking over my body and I busted a hard nut inside the condom.

After the great elevator sex, we put our clothes on and cuddled up in the corner falling asleep. After about three hours, a jerk from the elevator abruptly woke us up. He banged on the door and I jumped to my feet and looked around forgetting I was in an elevator. I looked down at Janet still slumped on the floor, shoes off bad legs open, and I laughed to myself. All of a sudden, I heard voices outside of the elevator. I woke Janet up and told her. We began to bang on the elevator to get whoever it was outside the doors attention. We spoke to the person outside the door and told them we'd been stuck for a while.

Within an hour, the elevator people came through and we were finally released from the elevator. We walked out of the elevator, looked at each other as Janet fixed her hair and walked out of the building to our cars. A week later, we signed our lease for the building. Janet and I fucked a few more times with no strings attached, Earl and I built our studio and the elevator got repaired. but I still use the steps hoping not to get "STUCK" again.

009. STUCK II

"Damn I still got to go see Laya," I said to myself thinking of my busy schedule. I promised Laya that I would come see her since the last two times I was home I didn't get a chance to kick it with her. Laya and I had been friends since elementary school and I knew her almost as we'll as I knew myself. For as long As I could remember Laya was the type of girl who always had her hair in ponytail, definitely wasn't a Barbie Doll type of girl and was into all the sports you could think of. In high school we were thick as thieves, I stayed over her house almost every weekend. A few nights she would sleep in boy shorts exposing her thick thighs and smooth brown legs and even though it was a mouthwatering sight unfortunately, I never touched her or thought of fucking her. I helped her get through her heartbreaks, first love, and even attended prom with her once her original ditched her. She was my home girl and I had her back like a spine.

After high school, we went our separate ways Laya stayed home an attended a community college, I on the other hand moved and went to school in Georgia. Every other day for a couple months straight we talked until our college lifestyle got between us and we grew apart, she got into a serious relationship and I spent most of my time smoking weed, drinking liquor and fuckin bitches. I thought of all of our memories and even laughed to myself a couple times as I drove to her mom's house. Between the bad weather and my thoughts running wild, a ride that would normally take me 10 minutes almost took me a half of an hour. Pulling into her mom's driveway I sat for a moment finished my thoughts and snapped back into reality.

"Hello," she answered the phone on the first ring.

"Lay I'm outside." I smiled into the receiver.

"Okay, here I come." I could hear the excitement in her voice.

"Alright!" I sat in the car for almost 5 minutes before I saw the door open and Laya walk onto the porch and motion for me to come in.

"What took you so long?" I laughed picking up a bit of snow, throwing her in a headlock and faked a motion as if I was going to smoosh it in her face.

"Shut up nigga I was in the shower."

"Good I'm happy you washed ya stankin ass," I said laughing as I walked into the house.

"So What's up ass hole? you haven't came to see me in almost two years I should smack you," she said laughing as I removed my coat and shoes.

"I've been busy man school..."

"Hoes," she interjected laughing at the same time.

"You been over here too busy for me to so who you foolin? Over here playin wifey and shit, And speaking of, you don't think your man will feel some type of way about me coming over here?"

She stood there and continued to smile as she shook her head. "No, he knows about you I talk about you all the time, I told him you was coming past."

"Oh okay, let me find put you be talkin bout me all the time punk." I smiled shaking my head at her. "Anyways where's Mrs.Frances?"

We took a few steps to make our way in the living room where the lights from the tall Christmas tree were shining brightly in the corner of the dark room.

"She's at a Christmas party at my step dad's job," Laya replied plopping down on the couch.

"Oh I know she's getting turned up, your mom is funny as fuck when she's drunk!"

She picked her phone up off the table then folded her legs Indian style. "Please don't remind me, she is so embarrassing."

"No she ain't I love her she cool as hell."

"Whatever you say Tone," she's rolled her eyes, "So how's that GA life? I know you got you a couple big booty hoes down there!" She was cracking herself up at her own joke barely being able to speak the words with a straight face.

" You think you're funny huh punk?" I put my arm around her neck and pulled her down. "It's cool though, it's definitely better than here and It will be way easier for me to find a job there after I graduate instead of moving back, plus it is a lot of big booty bitches down there and you know they be lovin the boy!" I laughed then continued watching some

Christmas movie that was on TV. "So, what's up with you Lil' Lay Lay? When you comin to Ga to turn up with a nigga?"

Hardly paying attention to what I was saying she scrolled down her Instagram news feed, "Hopefully one day when I'm free on a weekend cause a bitch definitely need to turn up and maybe I'll find me a lil shorty while I'm down there." she laughed looking up from her phone.

"A shorty huh?" I looked at her with a smirk on my face. " You know you aint never leavin that nigga you with especially as long as you wanna stay in the latest gear and rockin the hottest bags." Laya wasn't the same girl she was on high school. Once she got older and her body started filling out she started attracting older niggas who gave her anything she wanted, changing her from a tomboy to a bombshell.

In the middle of speaking her phone rang "Speak of the devil it's my boyfriend, do you care if I pick up?"

"No, why would I care? Answer your phone!"

"Hey baby." She spoke into the phone seductively as if she wasn't just talkin shit. "Nothing sitting here with Tone, remember I told you about my best friend from high school?" Her nigga obviously wasn't feelin the situation as I collected bits n pieces of her conversation but trying to pretend I wasn't listening. "I swear I told you he was coming over... she's at a party with Mr. Martin...nothing we're just sitting here talking that's it... it's nothing like that bae he's like my brother.... ok I'm not about to argue with you I'll talk to you later." She hung up the phone and rolled her eyes.

"I knew that nigga wasn't gon be cool with me being here! Niggas don't be Tryna here that friend shit!"

"Well he need to stop 'cause I don't want ya ass and he knows that!" Just as she rolled her eyes the phone rang again. "It's my mom."

"Oh let me answer your phone!"

"Hey Mrs.Frances!"

"Hi, Who's this answering my daughter's phone, is this Darrell?"

"No no no this is Tone! You mean to tell me you don't know my voice Mrs. Fran? And I thought I was your favorite!"

"Ohh, Tone how you doing baby?" She said with a slight slur. "You are my favorite baby you know that! I don't know why Lay don't just marry you and leave these other little hood rats alone!" I couldn't help but to smile with the phone glued to the side of my face.

"I been good just trying to graduate school...but your funny Mrs. Fran you know I can't marry that crazy girl I know too much about her," I said chuckling.

"Mark my words baby y'all gon get married," she said laughing, "But anyways how's your mom? Tell her I said hi and Merry Christmas!"

"She's good and I'll definitely tell her! She'll be happy to hear it."

"I know so don't forget to tell her! It's been a long time! where's my daughter?"

"She's right here. It was nice talking to you Mrs. Fran here goes Laya." I handed the phone to Laya.

"Lay bay! I don't think I'm gonna make it home tonight you see how bad it is out there?" Her mom blared into the phone causing Laya to open the curtains behind us to glance out the window.

"Oh my God Tone look!" I glanced out the window as well to see what the commotion was about. The streets and sidewalks were crystal white and my car was completely covered.

"Damn, I might be staying here tonight, ask your mom can I stay."

"Where else would you be going ass? Plus, you know that whip
Of yours ain't makin it nowhere in that kind of snow anyway," she said laughing then continued speaking to her mom, " Alright ma be safe and I'll see you tomorrow when the roads clear up...love you too...ok...goodnight ma!"

Hours flew past as we reminisced about out child hood, highschool and college life all while taking a few shots in between.

"Remember you came to Walmart with my me and my mom and we hid in them clothing racks, then hopped out the middle when people was looking through the clothes." I laughed hysterically bringing up memory after memory.

"Yes, I remember. You damn near killed that poor old lady when you poked your head out that rack, I never in my life seen a old white lady run that fast, " she said busting out laughing.

242

"She definitely dropped that cane fast as hell and dipped down the aisle but the look on her face was priceless you would have thought she saw a terrorist or something!"

"That's crazy, we was terrible" She shook her head
"I know man we did so much shit, you remember I tried to lock my parents in the basement like that movie "House Arrest" them white kids made it seem cool to lock their parents in basement."
"Yeah until your dad came up there and body slammed that ass! Man why was we so reckless?" She said still cracking up laughing. "I felt bad for you after he whooped your ass, he was hitting you hard as hell you looked like you was about to die, crying and shit snot coming down your nose like a lil punk!" She said Tryna clown.
"Man fuck you! That shit hurt," I said still laughing. "My dad is mad crazy."
"Anyways, Guess who I seen a couple days ago at the mall?"
"Who?"
"Omar! this nigga tried to get on me in the food court, he's a straight bum now I really can't believe I was fucking with his dusty ass back then."
"Man, I feel that same way about Amber, when I see her pictures on Instagram I be thinking what the fuck was I thinking?"
"That's exactly what I thought when I seen him, ugh he makes me sick to my stomach, all that money his family had and he's a dust ball."

"Isn't his mom a doctor and his dad in construction?

"Yes, they took his range Rover last summer 'cause he kept depending on his people too much."

"That's sad as hell yo," I said with a chuckle and glancing over at Laya as she was glued to her phone.

"Ugh, my boyfriend still tripping about you being over here."

"You want me talk to him?" I scratched the back of my head not knowing what else to say.

"No, he'll be okay, he don't usually act like this, he's being really weird right now."

"Where dude from?" I asked

"He's from the west side, he kind of remind me of you, chocolatey, tall and handsome."

"I never knew you thought I was handsome but thanks," I said flashing my gap-toothed smile.

"Don't get happy nigga you aight." She cleaned up her compliment.

"Whatever! I'm surprised your tomboy ass like niggas anyway," I said laughing.

"Shut up!" She mushed me in my head. "I'm better now I ain't that tomboy you know from grade school and high school I'm a lady now."

"Kiss me then so I know you really like niggas," I said with a little smirk and side eye. I couldn't believe I was taking things this route, but I guess the shots we took were starting to catch up. She looked me in the eyes and sat her phone on the middle table.

"Quit playing du..."

In the middle of speaking, I interrupted her

244

and I leaned over and cuffed the back of her head with the right hand, I kissed her lips twice then our tongues tied like ribbons. When our mouths detached we eyeballed each other for a few seconds, the expression on her face was somewhat shocked but then again, she looked like a lion that was ready to pounce on its dinner. I leaned towards her and got back to kissing her sexy lips. My mind was screaming, ***"No, stop, don't do this!"*** But my little man was telling me something totally different, and he was winning!

My kisses grew more intense and I pushed her back into the crease of the couch. I ran my tongue up her neck to the earlobe and listened while she moaned quietly with her mouth wide open. One thing led to another and before I knew it I was removing her shirt and working my way down to kissing her breasts. I reached my right arm around her back to pop the bra snap. Without delay the bra fell from her plump 38C sized breast onto her lap. I grabbed the left one then I wrapped my lips around her sugar brown nipple and I wiggled my wet tongue around it. I showed the right one the same attention as the left then I kneeled to my knees as I gradually licked down to her pelvis and licked across her panty line. Soon as I began to pull, her leggings off she pushed me back and removed them herself. As crazy as it seemed I think we were both more eager to feel each other than we ever thought we'd be.

I rolled my tongue up her right inner thigh then licked her panties in between her thighs so she could feel my tongue rubbing against her pussy. I slid the panties to the side with my index finger as I wrapped my lips around her clitoris, I built saliva in my mouth as I sucked and slid my tongue back and forth at a constant speed. As I got more into it, her panties just became a distraction and got in the way so I stopped licking for a few seconds, pulled them off then gripped both ankles, and pushed her legs far back towards her head. She looked down at me as I looked down to get a clear glimpse of her pretty nice shaved pussy all while still thinking I can't believe whose pussy I was actually looking at, my Lay lay. Snapping back into reality, I licked my lips and dove back into her wet pussy. She moaned with anticipation as I wrapped my lips around the clitoris and licked furiously while I shook my face side to side. She gripped the back of my head and moaned with a sexy tone in her soft voice

"Mmmmm, mmmmm!" Her moans just set me off more as I made wet slurping and sucking noises while eating the fuck out of her tasty vagina. She moaned in ecstasy as she began to fuck my face, pushing her pussy against my lips. Her facial expression and body movement gave me a sign that she was on the verge of cumming. I kept the pace and continued to use the same techniques on her and in no time her body got stiff, her back arched off the couch as she yelled out,"Ohhhhhhhh shiitttttt!" I kept throwing the neck, moving my lips with the steady pace of her thrusting her pussy on my face,

"Ohhhhh! Fuck fuck fuck!" she wailed out as her juices dripped down my lips to the hair on my chin, my tongue still moving nonstop while she gripped my head tighter and tighter continually yelling out " I'm CUMMMINGGGGG!" until her juices exploded on my face and her body loosened like a floppy noodle.

"You like that huh?" I wiped my mouth with the sleeve of my sweatshirt and stared at her with a cocky grin.

"Shut up and come up here and give me some dick! You got a condom?" She glanced down at me as I laid my head on her right thigh. She didn't say nothing but a word I was all for stroking her soul, I reached down in my pockets and pulled the gold package out.

"You know I do." I removed my jeans, ripped the wrapper then stretched the rubber down my thick nine-inch rock hard black dick, as she reached for the remote control her eyes opened wide.

"Oh my God that thing is big!" She turned the television off and gave me all her attention. "I don't know if I can handle that thang."

"Turn around, I'll go slow." The Christmas lights from the tree and the lights in the windows were the only lights shining. Laya turned around with her knees on the pillows and face towards the back cushion of the couch. I admired her standing there with her ass in the air as I stood behind her and spread her cheeks for easier access. I plunged my dick in her warm wet pussy and listened to her give put a loud moan and try to run at the same time. I moved my dick in and out of her at a slow steady pace to give her time to get adjusted. Once she started moving her hips to the pace of my humps, I began to apply pressure to the middle of her back with my right palm to arch her spine while I held my other hand over the Chinese lettering tattoo on her shoulder. I pulled her body in closer to mine as I began to speed up my pace some. Her moans got louder each time I threw my dick in her.

"Ohhhhhhhh oh oh mmmmm!"

The more she moaned the faster I increased the pace.

"Yes! Yes! Ohh Shit baby!"

In no time I felt like Laya was ready to get entertained, I gripped her chin and pushed her back down with more pressure; then I yanked her body into mines as I dug my dick into her pussy. Aggressively beating it down our skin collapsed together Making smacking noises.

"Owwwwww uh uh uh," she moaned.

Her ass jiggled as her long ponytail bounced with every stroke. She held onto the back of the couch gripping tightly, as I dove in. I pulled my penis out then snatched her wrist to pull her into a standing position.

"Come here, sit on the armrest"

Cooperatively she sat on the edge of the armrest, I stood between her legs and pulled her body near mines, I put my dick back inside as I grabbed each thigh and she wrapped her arms around my neck to prevent from falling back. Stroking and stroking her

248

juices fell onto the arm of the couch as she moaned in my ear giving me more motivation by letting me know she was enjoying herself.

"I . Love . This . Fuck . ing . Dick . Mmmmm . Fuck . Me .Fuck Me . Oh . My . Goshhhh . Like that like that. Yesss Mmmm!"

I adjusted her legs and put them straight up over my shoulders, she let go of my neck and flopped backward onto the couch with her ass remaining on the armrest. I watched as her stomach sunk In and out with every stroke as I watched her hands randomly moving to get a hold of a pillow to smoother her face with while she wailed into it. As I constantly pounded her pussy giving her all my dick.

No lie this pussy was feeling so fucking good I had to stop myself from saying I love you! I felt like a bitch but the pussy gave me chills, my eyes closed tightly and I was stopping myself from moaning as I continued to slam my dick inside of her. I knew she was loving every bit of this from the way her body quivered.

"Mmmmm Mmmm shiitttttt shit shit!" She yelled out breathing heavily. "Shit shit shit shit!" she threw the pillow at my head like a pitcher at a baseball game.

"Fuccccck!" she screamed as she pushed her legs off me, crawling back.

After cumming on my dick, she laid on the couch with her hands over her face. "What the hell are you doing to me?"

I ignored her question, spread her legs and dove face first into her pussy. Within minutes her body shook like she was having seizure, I kept my face in the pussy and continued licking as saliva mixed with her nut dripped down my chin hairs.

"Stop, stop, stop" she said as she locked my face in between her thighs, squeezing the shit out my head "what the fuck! Owwww," she moaned.

I didn't give her any time to recuperate I sat on the couch with a rock hard dick in my palm.

"Get up I want you to sit on it!" Without any hesitation, she got up, climbed over my lap facing the same direction I was facing and slowly went down the dick like an elevator. I reclined back and laid my hands on her soft brown ass as she bounced up and down with her hands on my knees. I smacked her ass with aggression as I used the floor for support pushing my toes off of it to lift my waist upward as she bounced down. I bit down on my bottom lip as I watched her ass drop up and down on my hard dick. Her moans got louder and louder as she held her hands on my knees and looked up at the ceiling. She bounced up and down on my dick slowing up a couple times to ride the head only then slammed back down on my dick causing nut to slowly creep up my dick.

"Oh shit, keep going, ride that dick," I said as she continued bouncing and bouncing on my dick.

"Here I cum, here I cum!" She screamed as I continued driving my penis up in her pussy and in no time I felt a chill run through my body as I let loose in the condom.

"Ummmm," I groaned, busting a nut as she dug her nails deep in the skin of my legs and wailed, "Mmmmmmmmm" draining her juices on my dick.

I pulled out and watched as Laya plopped her body down on the couch. I scratched the back of my head as guilt quickly took over my mind. Still sitting there butt naked but in shock and feeling hella weird I couldn't help but to ask,

"How did this happen?"

"I don't know Tone this is kind of weird and I got a damn boyfriend." She glanced back at me with hair coming out the ponytail.

"I know, shit I've known you forever and we never fucked, I hope this don't get in between our friendship."

"It won't," She spoke standing up and picking up her clothes from the floor. "But honestly you fucked me way better than my man, I haven't got sex like that in a..."

Boom boom boom! Her sentence interrupted by a knock at the door. I jumped off the couch my heart jumping out my chest.

"Oh shit!!" I said scrambling to grab hold of my clothes. Laya turned the TV on and together we got dressed in a hurry.

"Omg what if that's Justin he always show up unexpectedly he's crazy as hell."

I sat back on the couch an acted like I was watching TV hoping that wasn't her nigga at the door. Things would be way to awkward sittin around that nigga after I just fucked his woman. Laya made her way to the door and quickly glanced through the peephole.

"Ohh it's just my sister."

10. WET BODIES

When I pulled into the parking lot of my apartment complex my phone rang flashing Tasha's name with heart emojis next to them.

"What up babe?" I answered the phone and pulled the key out the ignition.

"Hey, How you doing baby?" she cooed with her soft sexy voice.

"I'm just getting home I'm exhausted for real."

"You sound like you had a rough day."

"Yeah, it felt longer than usual; I had to load the truck with bricks all day." I rubbed my forehead for a brief second mentally recapping my day.

"Well, if you still want me to come over I can rub your back when I get there, and I know you won't feel like cooking do you want me to get you something to eat?"

I completely forgot I told her to come over. Although, I had other plans with Asia dinner and a massage sounded too good. "Yeah, I still want you to come over." I spoke opening the door to my apartment.

"Okay, do you work tomorrow?"

"Yeah at 9, why? Are you staying?"

"If you want me to." I knew she was smiling on the other end. I could hear it in her voice as I kicked off my work boots.

"You can I don't mind." The feeling of walking without the boots felt like I was stepping on heaven's clouds.

"I'm just leaving the gym can I please take a shower over there?"

"I don't even know why you even ask, as many times you been over here."

"I guess that's a yes."

"I'm not saying anything else call me when your close."

"Okay baby."

I flopped on the couch, reclined back, then reflected on life as I sat comfortably. In no time my eyelids closed, my body shut down on me like a car that burned out of gas from working twelve-hour shifts for two weeks straight.

My phone rang, rudely waking me up out a good ass nap and I jumped up noticing Tasha's name on the screen.

"Yooo," I answered with a raspy voice still half-asleep.

"Were you sleep?"

"I dosed off real quick. Where you at?"

"Well, I'm on 28 I should be there in ten minutes. I got you some Jamaican food from Federal Street."

"Oh word, what you get?"

"I know you like curry chicken, so I got you that and red beans and rice and fried cabbage."

"Good look babe I appreciate that. I'm about

to straighten my apartment up real quick then hop in the shower. Just in case I'm in the shower when you get here I'mma keep the door unlocked, okay."

"Okay baby."

In the kitchen, I put the dishes in the dish washer, vacuumed the living room floor and stacked the pillows neatly in their places. I found some girl's earrings in between the seat cushion of the couch and tossed them in the lost and found drawer in my bedroom that I stored female's lost items in. My bedroom was a mess. Clothes were everywhere but in the drawers and in the close and my shoes were out the boxes. I could've pushed everything under the bed but I'm not 10 years old, instead I balled the clothes up one by one and stuffed them in the dressers, I placed my shoes in the boxes then stacked the boxes of shoes in the closet.

As I finished cleaning, the music stopped and my phone rang. I grabbed my phone, hurried to the bathroom, turned the bathwater on then I answered. Hello."

"I'm at the light I'll be there in a minute."

"Alright, just come in I'm in the shower." I ended the phone call, the music on Pandora resumed to play, I removed my work uniform, socks and boxer briefs then stepped in the shower.

The hot steamy water dripped down my face running down my chocolate body; I soaked the rag with soap then washed my face first, scrubbed my arm and swiped across the tattoos on my chest. The bubbles slid down to my pubic hairs as the water ran against my upper body.

As I began to soak the rag with more soap to clean my lower body Tasha slid the shower curtain to the side, poking her head in the shower
"Hey babe."

She caught me spontaneously. My soul ran out my skin as the soap slid out my fingertips, falling onto the tub floor-sliding pass my toes. All I saw was her brown face with her hair in a sweaty ponytail. "OH SHIT, YO!" I said as I jumped frightened.

"See I got you dropping the soap, pick it up so I can smack your butt." She giggled, being goofy.

I didn't think that shit was funny. "Ha ha you got jokes, nah you come in here and pick it up, fucking creeping up on me."

"I thought you heard me come in."

"The music was loud as hell for real."

"Sorry, I didn't mean to scare you." she said still giggling.

"I got you one day, I'm cool punk."

She got quiet for a second; I slid the curtains to the left to catch of glimpse of what she was doing. My mouth dropped as I watched her bend over to dig in a gym bag to get clothes. The view was beautiful she had hot pink gym leggings on showing curves like a windy road, my dick grew like a tree with Miracle Grow.

"What you doing?" I ask.

"I'm getting my towel and rag out; I didn't bring any sleeping clothes so I'll be sleeping in my undies."

"You should've asked if I had towels and rags, if you want to wear a t-shirt you can wear one." I shut the shower curtain back

"Aww thanks babe, well I'm about to get in the shower with you, you better not try nothing nasty, we know how you are."

"Come on, I'm not gonna touch unless you want me to." Lies escaped my lips. "I'm not the nasty one that's you." I slid the curtain to take another look. She was in panties and a sport bra, she had a rose vine tattoo that started from her ass going up the side of her rib. Slowly she removed her panties sliding them down her smooth brown legs then removed her bra revealing her nice pair of D titties. Her nipples were pierced with gold bows and arrows, when she stepped toward the tub I hurried and shut the curtain.

"You're a pervert, I seen you looking the whole time."

"What you talking about I was fixing the curtain?" I acted incognizant.

The water ran down her body; hitting her neck and back as she faced me. "Whatever nigga."

"What? I'm not allowed to look? Here wash my back." I handed the rag and soap over to her, and then turned around.

"You are, but the face you were giving me while you were staring…" She gently rubbed the soapy rag across my neck.

"Mmh that feels good." She continued to run the rag down my back before washing my arms.

"Your butt is all stiff and black." Tasha giggled and smacked my ass in a joking matter.

"Yo, chill." I quickly turned around and snatched the rag off her.

"Aww did I make you mad, babe?" She continued to laugh.

"No just don't be touching my butt, let me get some water its getting cold back here." While the water rained down on me she was soaping her titties, washing down her thighs, she lifted her leg up on the edge of the tub and began to clean between them.

"Now can you wash my back she" she asked.

"Yeah, I got you." With the rag I began to wash from her lower back then up the spine; by the time I got to her shoulders my dick was hard, and pointing directly towards her. If my dick had a hand, it probably would've snatched her up itself. I couldn't resist kissing her neck; for some odd reason her neck was very appealing to me, she had a tattoo in the back of her neck that read "Est. 1989" and on the right side of her neck were red kissy lips.

I sat her rag on the soap holder then began to massage her shoulders as the soap ran clear off her back. I kissed all over her neck she stepped back letting a moan escape her lips.

"Why is your dick hard?" she asked staring at my dick poking her on the ass cheek.

"I don't know you got him like that."

"Oh I got him like that?" She reached back with the left palm then squeezed my dick. Twisting her wrist, she began to stroke my hard black dick at a mild steady pace.

"Dammmmnnn babe that shit feels good," I said as she continued to stroke, water from the shower streamed down her arms and wrist while she jerked my hard meaty dick.

She turned towards me then pecked my lips. "See what you started," she whispered.

"Be quiet." I kissed the side of her neck, ran the tip of my tongue up and across her throat as her beautiful head went back and mouth opened, moaning while my tongue slid across her pretty lips. I grabbed her chin firmly with my working hands then brought her face towards mine, our lips reconnected, our tongues twisted against one another as I cuffed my free hand on her breast. The kissing lasted no longer than twenty seconds I had a taste for something sweeter. I pushed her back against the steamy white towels on the wall, lifted her sexy legs up by the thigh to force her to put her feet on the corner of the tub. I kneeled down, the water falling on top of my head going down my back. I wrapped my lips around her clit, gently I sucked then swiped my tongue across it like a bad credit card. She gripped the back of my head as the tone of her moan became louder. I slid my tongue back and forward giving her clit my undivided attention, I licked motivated by her "Mmmmmm baby," wails.

Licking sucking and licking sucking, shaking my face all in between her delicious pussy as the hot water sprayed our bodies. She forcefully pulled my face in, yanking the back of my head as her leg got stiff like dry Playdough.

"Ohhh shittt baaaby," she's moaned.
I kept licking and licking smacking that clit at a constant pace.

"Ohh shit oh shit, oh shit!" She moaned with a sexy tone in her voice. She closed her eyes tight, as she got weak in the knees; her breathing was heavy as I made her pussy burst.

I didn't give her a chance to recuperate, soon as I stood to my feet I bent her over and I grabbed hold of her neck then plugged my dick between the lips of her pussy slowly pushing it in. She gasped for air as inches of dick went deep in her. Stroking in and out I was digging and digging all inside her as her hands slid on the steamy tile walls.

"Mmmmh mmmmh!" Her moans gradually got louder in the time I increased the pace of my stroke. I watched my dick slide in and out while her ass jiggled and titties bounced from the penetration. My left hand gripped her shoulder, right hand on the upper thigh. I pulled her body into mine while I struck her with my powerful black dick. The water splashed uncontrollably falling outside of the tub making the shower curtain useless. the shower curtain didn't help much. When our bodies met the noise sounded like we were having a face slapping contest.

"Mmmm shit shit shit shit babbby!" Her moan got louder as I was throwing the dick in with force as I continued to pull her body into me. Tasha moaned to every stroke and the water ran down my face like sweat.

She slid the shower certain to the side then stepped out and glanced at me with a grin on her face. Her hair was wet and curly, I stepped out the shower behind her with water dripping off my skin. As I sat on the toilet top, she smiled with that same grin on her face as she held my dick upward. She stepped over me, sat down on the tip then slowly went down.

"This feels way better than being in the shower." I thought to myself. I could feel her warm wet pussy lips swallow my dick whole.

"Mmmmh," she wailed as she bit her bottom lip.

I planted my feet on the wet floor as she gradually bounced on my dick. I pushed upwards every time she came down.

"Oh, baby, I, love, love this dick," she screamed as I continued driving my dick up in meeting her halfway.

"Cum on this dick, cum on the mothafucking dick," I'm saying as I grip onto her ass.

She changed motions; rocking back and forward, I choked her with one hand and the opposite hand I kept a good hold of her ass to pull her lower body toward my abs. She looked up with her mouth wide open and eyes closed.

"Cum on this DICK cum on this DICK!" I kept pushing like the Salt and Pepper song. She wrapped her arms around my neck and squeezed tight.

"Cum on this dick, cum all on this shit," I'm demanding

The way she's rocking on me I felt the toilet seat about to break with the loose screws that held the seat in place. It didn't interrupt us. She rocked and rocked on this dick moaning and screaming in ecstasy. Tasha squeezed even tighter.

"Oh shiiiittt I'm cumming!"

I wrapped my arms around her back like book bag strap and pulled her down on the dick while she melted all over my dick.

I wrapped my arms around her back as if they were the straps of a backpack, pulling her down on the dick while she melted all over it. I felt her pussy throbbing and her body shaking. She grinned at me, like she was going to do something sneaky.

"I want that dick in my mouth." She stood up then dropped to her knees. She wrapped her hand around my dick and spit on the cone of it. The saliva was streaming down my dick to my balls, as she slowly stroked; up and down while she twisted her wrist.

"Damn!" I said, as I glanced down.   She opened her mouth and sucked and beat my dick at the same time. Her mouth and hands were putting in teamwork. I was running my fingers through her wet hair while trying to push down on her head. My toes curled. My legs stiffened.

"Mmmm, cum for me daddy," she mumbled as it slid in and out of her mouth. She was determined to make me nut. As Tasha bobbed her head faster and faster, I heard a knock at the door.

Knock, knock, knock! She was still sucking and stroking on my dick. I'm not even sure if she heard anything. *Boom, boom, boom.*

"OPEN THE FUCKING DOOR DRE!"

Tasha lifted her head up, but kept her wet hand on my dick. "You hear that?" She finally spoke. "Who's that banging at ya door?"

I jumped up with guilt on my mental. "I don't know. This one chick."

"Why this girl even here?"

Boom, boom, boom! "OPEN THE FUCKING DOOR! I KNOW YOU'RE HERE! YOUR CAR IS IN THE PARKING LOT!" Asia banged on the door harder this time. I thought she was going to break the door.

"Here, put this around you." I handed Tasha a towel before making my way into the living room naked. Every step I took my dick swung side to side, and I left wet tracks on the carpet. I peeked out the peephole and saw her big, shiny, light-skinned forehead. "***Why do the chicks with big foreheads seem to always be delightful to the eyes?***" I smiled thinking to myself. Her hair was in a ponytail, as she stood there furious. The flames were burning in her brown eyes.

"DRE! OPEN THIS FUCKING DOOR!"

I glanced back staring at Tasha with the towel wrapped tightly around her body looking confused and nervous.

"Who is this girl Dre?" she asked again.

"Her name is Asia. We mess around, but she ain't my girl or nothin'. We just be fuckin." I peeked out the peephole and answered in a whisper. Asia quickly resorted to banging on my door and ringing my phone.

"So you're fuckin' her too?" she asked.

"We fucked a few times but you can't be mad because we ain't together, plus you have a girlfriend." I yelled back. Suddenly it went silent scaring me to the point that I was hesitant to glance out the peephole. My mouth dropped as Asia picked up a brick. I quickly sprinted to the room walking past Tasha as if she wasn't there.

"What are you about to do? Are you letting her in?" Tasha asked in awe as I reached in the drawer for my gray sweat pants.

"No! But this bitch is about to brick my car." I ran to the door as I hopped to pull my pants up. I slid my slippers on then opened the door. Asia had the burnt orange brick in the palm of her hand seconds from releasing her rage on my driver's side window. "HOLD ON! HOLD ON YO! What the fuck is your problem?"

"Ha! Oh now you wanna come out huh? You must have a bitch in your house?"

"Man, put the brick down." At this point, the nosey old white neighbors across the street were watching us like a movie from the Redbox.

"You're always stringing me along. You told me the other day, you wanted to be with me and you loved me."

"I know what I told you...But, I also told you I wasn't ready to be committed. So, put that brick down man." I stepped closer as I spoke.

"Sooo do you got company? Do you have company?" She scowled still not putting the brick down.

"Yes, I do."

"Oh, well I want to meet her" She dropped the brick and folded her arms across her chest as she walked towards me.

"Man, I'm not letting you up there so you can tear my apartment up." I held her back as she attempted to cross my path. She pushed me with force determined to get past me.

"I want to see what this bitch looks like. I need to see if she looks better than me, Shit, I might want to fuck her since you're fucking her already!"

"Chill yo, I'm not gonna let you up there. Just get in the ride and take your ass home!" I continued to push her back.

"Oh, you care about this bitch that much that you won't let me in your apartment?" She spoke as her fist punched the air. Immediately, I grabbed her wrist to stop her from swinging.

"Man, chill the fuck out! Calm your ass down. You're making a fool of yourself." I was so frustrated at this point that I wanted to smile as the craziest thought crossed my mind. ***"They both fuck with females, so why not introduce her to Tasha?"***

"Do you really want to meet her?" I questioned knowing there was no getting out of this.

"Yes. I'm not going hurt your little girlfriend." She huffed scowling at me acting shocked I didn't trust her crazy.

"She ain't my girl and I swear you better not snap when you get in my apartment."

"I won't! Look at you all scared I'm going to beat your bitch up." She smiled walking up the stairs with me behind her.

"Nah, I don't want you fucking up my crib, we both know you're good for destroying shit."

"Like what?" she smacked her lips offended.

"Don't act stupid. You threw my phone at my flat screen and broke them both. And, you were just about to brick my car. Shit, you're lucky I still fuck with you."

Asia rolled her eyes still not seeing my view of things. "No, you're lucky I still fuck with your ass always sending mixed signals."

"I don't send mixed signals, you just be hearing what you want to hear." I said, as we stepped in the apartment. Asia walked in behind me, then dramatically sniffed.

"It smells like sex in here."

I laughed and walk towards the bedroom door. "You're saying anything. Sit down while I talk to her."

"Oh, you're buying bitches' food now? I can't even get McDonalds! You're so worried about pleasing these hoes out here, when I'm the one who been down for you since day one."   Asia spotted the food Tasha bought me sitting on the coffee table in the living room.

"Shut up before I put you back outside." I yelled straightening my face before twisting the knob on the bedroom door. I shut the door behind me and stared at Tasha seated on the edge of the bed showing no type of emotion. She was looking fine in her boy shorts and bra. I would've thought she'd be fully dressed and ready to leave because of the situation I put her in but I guess I was attracted to crazy. I cleared my throat before speaking. "So… I brought Asia up here to meet you."

"I heard. I was listening from the window."

I glanced over at the window and noticed the blinds were down in the middle. "Well, I'm not going anywhere. My plans were to stay the night, cuddle with you and fuck throughout the night. I don't care what she does but I'm staying and you're going to give me what I want. I'm not getting bullied out this house."

I scratched my forehead in awe as I sat next to her. "I'll have her go home. I just want you to meet her real quick."

"Why should I?" she spoke twisting her face.

"Just one time for me? Maybe she'll go away."

"No, I don't want to meet no one you're fucking. Get her out the house! I want to finish what we started!" She almost whined staring me in my eyes.

"Alright." I stood up and made my way out the bedroom and shut the door behind me. "She said she don't want to meet anyone, you're going have to go home."
"Why can't she leave?" Asia now whined poking her lip out.

"I'm not making her leave because you came. I attempted to have you two meet, which should be enough."

"Okay okay, I'll leave." She stood to her feet and walked towards the front door.
"What are you doing?" As soon as I slid my slippers on she dropped directly to her knees and pulled my dick out my sweat pants. I pushed her forehead back then covered my dick with both hands. She licked the brown side of my hand and ran her tongue across my wrist. *"I was definitely attracted to crazy,"* I thought to myself as she covered my middle finger with her

lips and sucked slowly. My dick was rising like the sun at 8am. She was sucking my finger so fucking good I couldn't resist. I released my hands and set my dick free, like a bird out of a cage. With no time to think and react to what the consequences were if Tasha decided to come out, Asia grabbed my dick and stuffed my big juicy dick in her mouth. "Oh, shit," I blurted out as I bit my bottom lip.

She soaked my dick with the first suck, leaving saliva all over it. She removed her mouth from my dick and began to stroke faster. At this point, I couldn't control my moans.

"Mmmmh mmmmh," in a low tone I wailed. She sucked and continued to beat my wet hard dick. "Mmmmmh mmmmmh...what the fuck?" The tone of my moan was higher. She was sucking my dick like there was no tomorrow. My toes curled in my slipper. My knees got weak, but I continued to watch her perform. The head was feeling so amazing. I didn't consider fucking up this fulfilling moment. I reached to put my hand over Asia's head and I heard the door swing open.

 "WHAT THE ACTUAL FUCK IS THIS?" Tasha asked with animosity in her voice.   Asia detached her mouth from my dick and her palm remained around it like she was marking her territory. I glanced back at Tasha and looked directly in her eyes, but I didn't break silence.

  "Don't act like you don't know what going on, I'm sucking his dick." Asia spoke sarcastically. She licked the tip of my dick then deep throated that shit. I pushed her forehead back to stop her.

"Yo chill real quick." She just started sucking my dick ignoring my instruction. "If you want to leave I understand. It's up to you."

"What did I tell you in the room?" Tasha raised her brow surprised I was offering her an out.

"You said you weren't leaving for no one."

Asia sucked and stroked my dick for a few seconds then removed her mouth. "Well bitch, I'm not leaving either. I've been fucking with him for over a year."

"I don't give a damn how long you two have messed around. Don't call me a bitch, you don't know me like that. And shorty, from my view, you ain't even suckin' his dick right."

"Well, he seemed to like it. Do you Dre?" Asia stared up at me.

"Don't put me in this yo," I refused to be caught in the middle.

Tasha chuckled before stepping forward with a devilish grin on her face. "Let me show you how to suck a man's dick." My dick throbbed as Tasha spoke those great words and dropped to her knees. She bumped Asia to the side with her elbows and snatched my dick off her like the flags in flag football.

"Give me this." Tasha insisted staring at Asia. Asia stared at her as if she had lost her damn mind and watched as Tasha licked the side of my dick with her thick wet tongue getting it completely moist. She cuffed my balls with her fingertips and wrapped her mouth around my long, thick, juicy, hard black curvy dick before sucking the fuck out of my dick.

My eyes rolled in the back of my head. "Ohh Shit! Oh shit! Damn!" I couldn't believe this shit was happening to me. I went from amazing shower sex to getting head by two females that had the potential to be my lady someday.   Not even a minute passed, and Asia grabbed my dick and pulled it out Tasha's mouth. She stuffed my dick in her mouth then went to work on it as well. She sucked and stroked and sucked and stroked my dick to the point my knees got weak. If this was a competition, they'd be neck and neck, because the neck both of them were throwing had me gone out my mind. They were determined to prove who's the ultimate dick sucker.

"How about ya'll share? Asia, you suck on the dick. And Tasha, you suck my balls." I suggested. As I glanced down,   Tasha's thick, wet tongue slid across my scrotum. Then she gently sucked as her tongue slid back and forth Asia kept sucking. She was bobbing her head with no hands involved. I put my hands over the back of both heads, just like I'd seen in a porn. As a matter of fact, I felt like a porn star the way these ladies were sucking the life out of me.

"Wait, wait. I want to taste the both of ya'll." Before I bust my nut, I stopped them in the act. "Come in the room." They sat beside each other on the bed but wouldn't speak or even look at one another. I guess they both were being petty. I didn't care how they were feeling I get on my knees and yanked Asia's boy shorts off. Then, I unbuttoned Tasha's tight pants and removed them as well.
 These women were looking like dinner and I was the beast, ready to devour. I spread Tasha's legs wide open, then licked up her inner thighs until I encountered her wet, juicy pussy. I filled my mouth with saliva, wrapped my lips around her clit, then slid my tongue back and forth across her clit as I sucked gently.

"Mmmmmh Daddy," she moaned as I continued to smack on her clit with my tongue but I paused for a second to shove my index and middle finger in my mouth to get my fingers nice and wet. My lips get reacquainted to Tasha's pussy as I reached over to play with Asia's pussy. My face was between Tasha's legs, so it was difficult to see. Treating her body like braille, I felt around until I found Asia's clit. When I got a good feel, I flicked my wrist side to side to stimulate her pussy. The more I swiped, I felt her pussy juices slowly pouring out.

Their moans were like music to my ears. Asia's moans were loud and high-pitched. While Tasha's were more curse words, whispering and loud breathing. Her "mmmm, shit and oh my God's" were the perfect melody. I switched bodies and begin to eat Asia. She liked her pussy eaten differently than Tasha. She hated when a man sucked her clit. I licked her clit before sticking my thick, juicy tongue inside her wet hole then sucking it; going in and out, while my top lip caressed her clit. I arched my index and middle finger then plugged the index into Asia's wet pussy and rubbed the ceiling of it playing with her g-spot. As I plugged her kitty, I plugged the middle finger in her tight ass hole then dipped in and out of both holes.

When I finished snacking on these ladies appetizing pussy I was ready to fuck, my dick was hard then a mothafucka. I crawled on the bed and laid back on the comfortable soft white comforter. I grabbed Tasha's ankle and placed her over my face. She was facing towards my feet as she sat straight up. While I stick my tongue in Tasha's ass I felt Asia adjusting herself over my dick as she held it in place to slide slowly down. Her pussy was wet and messy, my toes curled as soon as the tip of my penis felt her pussy lips hugging my dick. Asia and Tasha were facing one another; Asia was riding the fuck out my dick like a new car full of gas as my tongue slipped in Tasha's pussy. I grabbed Tasha's fat ass then began to bounce her pussy on my tongue. The bed was squeaking, they both were moaning from the top of their lungs, I could feel the breeze from the cracked window blow as I pleased these women. I bet the nebby neighbors were listening I wouldn't be surprised if the standing right by my car.

After a good ten minutes, we rearranged positions. I stood to my feet on the side of bed and pulled Tasha to the edge to have her ass hang off, Asia was sitting on her knees next to Tasha kneeling over her pussy sucking and stroking my dick making my meat extra wet. Before I could even stick my dick inside Tasha, Asia pulled my dick, plugged it in Tasha's pussy then began to suck on her brown pretty nipples. "***That's what I'm talking about team work***," I thought to myself.

I stroked between Tasha's thighs and pushed every inch of this dick in her while moving inside her with a steady pace as Asia rubbed Tasha's clit at the same time. In minutes, Tasha was tapping out.

"I'm about to cum," she screamed. I kept on stroking her soul because if I stopped she could lose a nut and in no time her body was frozen. "I'm cummin, I'm cummin!" Her body lifted up from the middle as she came all over my dick. I pushed my dick in her and kept it in her while she unraveled.

I fucked Asia from the back as Tasha got herself together, in no time she came as well.

The both of them kneeled to their knees and sucked my dick until I bust a huge nut all over their titties. Now they were both my girlfriends.

11. SEX FOR FORGIVENESS

If she's a good woman stay true to her cause most of these ladies ain't shit. You might leave the North Pole to move to Atlanta for better weather but get stuck in an ice storm. What I'm saying the grass isn't always greener on the other side. I rewrote the beginning of this story to tell you make up sex only works a few times but when a woman is fed up with the cheating and lying it's not going to fix anything. In relationships arguments are supposed to happen that's what builds the love, if your significant other leaves you for some bullshit then the love was never there, argue, make up and fuck.

I can't tell you our relationship was perfect, I can't say that I haven't made mistakes, I can't say our opinions on certain things always match, I can't say she didn't get on my nerves at times but what I can say is we were working shit out and that I loved this woman and I wasn't going nowhere.

"So, is this your excuse for coming in late last night?" Lisa quickly opened the shower curtain exposing my naked body.

Damn, I thought to myself while quickly searching my brain for an excuse, I was caught red handed and for the first time at a loss for words.

"It really ain't nothing she's just some chick

that work with me babe, that's it! And why are you going through my phone anyways?" I quickly turned off the water and wrapped the towel around my waist.

"Cause I can Mike! You told me you were at the bar with Brad, but obviously, that wasn't the case now was it? Got bitches texting you talking bout they had a good time last night! I should slap the dog shit out of you but it's not even worth it! So, what you do fuck that bitch?"

"No, she was at the bar we talked and had a drink I swear I wasn't fuckin around!"

"You're lying I can see the lies in your face nigga, here take your phone with your cheating ass," she said tossing the phone at my chest.

"Mannnnnn I wasn't chea…" I said as I tried to catch the phone and watched it fall face down onto the floor. She walked out the bathroom with her nose up as I instantly bent over to pick it up praying it wasn't cracked. "WHAT THE FUCK!" I screamed in anger looking at my cracked screen. I marched angrily behind her into the bedroom, "YOUR WEIRD AS FUCK FOR THROWING MY PHONE! YOUR DUMBASS WILL BE BUYING ME A NEW ONE."

"NO, YOU'RE WEIRD AS FUCK, I been loyal to you for years and you constantly fucking up our relationship for these hoes, you done so much shit to me I always take you back and you still got me sitting around looking stupid."

"Man, what the fuck," I screamed still fiddling with my phone not paying what she was saying a bit of attention!

"That's what you get; hopefully this will stop you from talking to your hoes so much."

"LISA!! I DON'T FUCK WITH THESE HOES, WHAT THE HELL!!! GIRLY HAPPENED TO BE AT RONNY'S THATS IT!!! THIS THE SHIT I'M TALKING ABOUT, NO TRUST, YOU DON'T TRUST A NIGGA FOR SHIT! I MINES WELL BE FUCKIN HOES I CAN'T EVEN GO TO THE STORE WITH OUT YOU QUESTIONING ME," I yelled getting my clothes on.

She stood up and stomped toward me until she was close enough to yell in my face, "HOW AM I SUPPOSED TO TRUST A NIGGA WHO CONTINUES TO CHEAT AND DISRESPECT ME AND THIS RELATIONSHIP, I'M TO THE POINT I DON'T EVEN CARE ANYMORE DO WHAT YOU DO! AND DON'T BE MAD WHEN I LEAVE YOUR SORRY ASS, I NEED A MAN WHO'S FOCUSED ON ME NOT THESE BITCHES!!" She scowled poking me in the chest meaning every word.

"Ok we'll since you don't give a fuck I'm out! And keep your fuckin hands off me! You're so fuckin insecure man I'm sick of that shit! "

"Obviously you don't care... about this... relationship... like I said .... You constantly cheat and cheat... I'm sick of the shit, that girl shouldn't even

278

have your number. I take shit from you that you would never take from me! You out here talking to these girls and entertaining the bullshit not thinking about your family at all! You say you love me but yet I'm constantly catching you doing shit."

"Stop fuckin pushing me! I'm done with this conversation, I don't know how she got my number, she might've got it from one of the co-workers, but I'm done with this. You don't trust me so whatever I say is a lie to you. Just leave me the fuck alone."

I could tell that she was hurt but I didn't know what to do but be defensive especially when I know I was wrong and there was nothing else to say.

She looked at me with so much hurt in her eyes, threw her hands up and backed up. "Okay, I'll leave you alone! I'm done with this shit anyway! I'm not a toy, I'm not a puppet you can't just do what you want to me! I don't see this getting any better so I'm giving up!"

"Ok we'll I'll stay at my moms this weekend!"

She didn't respond after I spoke but I know the way I was acting was doing nothing but hurting her more. I kept my composer cause I was over the whole situation, I could've confessed and apologized but I couldn't! And on top of it all my phone was broken and uninsured and I was pissed!

Regrets and Thoughts

Soon as I finished getting dressed, I walked into the kitchen to grab a bottle of water. I stood there drinking my water still thinking about how I could spruce up this situation and make myself look less guilty. I couldn't lie I felt bad as I sat and watched Lisa on the couch sitting Indian style holding back tears and trying to pretend as if she wasn't just gossiping about me on the phone. Still feeling guilty, I walked through the house like nothing happened. I grabbed a couple outfits and a couple pair of shoes. I didn't want to leave but I damn sure didn't want to argue either!

"Bye I'll see you Monday," I said nonchalantly, slamming the door behind me, knowing damn we'll I didn't really want to leave!

I drove and drove still thinking about and praying that I didn't fuck my relationship up for good this time! I didn't want to lose her and although I acted like a complete asshole, I cared more then she knew! All she ever did was love me and for some reason I couldn't stop fucking up! I thought about it until I finally made it to the mall to pick up a new phone. In the process, I browsed through the mall and bought myself a couple things to relieve my stress. I picked up some food from the food court, stopped past the liquor store and made my way over to my nigga Brad's crib. I couldn't get to Brad's quick enough! My mind was racing, and I needed a drink ASAP! I made my drink then went and sat on the couch to sip on a Henny with ice and scrolled through her Instagram and Facebook checking to see if she posted something. Lisa hadn't called or texted me since I left which was not normal for her. "She must be fed up for real this time." I thought to myself noticing she hadn't even posted on her social sites. Brad pressed pause on the PlayStation then blew marijuana smoke out his mouth as he glanced back.

"You cool man," he asked looking back at me.

"I'm good bra, just getting my thoughts together."

"You been quiet since you been here, Lisa got you over here buggin my nigga."

"It's not that I'm buggin but that's my girl yo, she a good woman I just keep fuckin up. She don't trust me for shit." He inhaled the smoke then resumed the game.

"That's wild bra I don't know how you do that relationship shit, niggas be stressing over these hoes, I fuck'em and keep it moving."

"I mean, you have your ups and downs, ain't no perfect relationships. Shit going happen y'all are going argue that's how relationships grows. My girl gets on my fucking nerves all the time, but I still love her."

He shook his head "Fuck that arguing shit, I'll put a bitch out on the door step and let her freeze, I don't be trying hear the bull shit."

I laughed hard as he'll as I lifted my glass and gulped another shot of my drink. "The way you're thinking you going be a lonely man living in your mama's basement playing PlayStation forever, ain't nothing wrong with being single my nigga but you can't play these women all your life, they'll get tired of you I'm telling you, plus a good woman can help you be a better and stronger man."

He puffed his blunt.

"How we go from talking about Lisa to talking about me? I'm just saying I'm not prepared for the bull shit when I love I love hard, when I feel I have the right woman then I'll cool it down but right now I'm living. You ain't ready your damn self. "
"What you mean by that?"
He paused the game and puffed on the weed
"Ol girl in the bar last night had your nose wide open, if her friends didn't cock block you would've left with her and probably would've fucked."

The Henny smoothly poured down my throat as I explained. "I was drunk as fuck, swear. She's my co-worker I told her about the spot earlier this week I honestly didn't know she was going come there but I should've known cause she's always tryna swerve."
"You was all in her face buying her drinks, kissing on her and shit but ol girl was sexy as fuck I don't blame you I would've been trying to fuck too if I was you"
"Shit, I must've gave Teresa my number in the mix too." I finished my drink then poured a double shot in the cup. "Man, I got to make shit right at home I can't run away from my problems plus I

can't sleep on this dirty ass couch anyways too many asses been on here. I'm bout to slide out bra."

I poured the shot in my mouth then slapped Brad hand. "Alright, sucker ass nigga," he said as he talked out the side his mouth with a blunt in the corner of his lips.

I grinned as I laughed. "It be like that."

...

When I walked in the house the lights in the hallway, living room and, kitchen were off and the house was pitch black. I walked through the house until I saw the only light on in the house and that came from the crack under the door in the bedroom, the house smelled like shrimp Alfredo and Dove soap. I heard music playing through the door as Lisa sang the words to the sad ass song. I slowly turned the knob and began to open the door slowly until I finally saw Lisa. She was in black cheeky panties and a matching bra; she sat in the middle of the bed with her back against the headboard as she slid her thumb on her phone. She didn't acknowledge that I came in at all! I felt like a ghost in the room as she continued to give the phone attention without showing any expression. I sat on the foot of the bed then glanced back and stared at her for a few seconds, I cleared my throat before speaking. " I'm sitting here because I want you to know I love you, I made a mistake I should of never gave shorty my number. I'm not going blame the alcohol, but I was drunk and I'm wrong!"

She continued to scroll through the phone like I wasn't saying shit all! She was curving me just how I did her earlier and I did not like the feeling. I continued to speak because I knew she was listening "I know you're upset this ain't the only time you caught me in some shit, I was only talking to the girl in the bar we didn't fuck or anything, it was just a friendly conversation. At work, I told her about the place because she's new in the city I really didn't know she was going to come plus she got nothing on my woman anyways so you don't got to worry about her. I mean you're mad but you're still over there looking sexy."

She looked up and continued to listen while I ran my mouth. "Even though you broke my phone I'm over it, your feelings are more important to me, I apologize."

She put her phone down and scowled at me.

"You're always apologizing. I'm so sick of your shit, I can't trust you far as I can throw you!! Then the bitch work with you that makes the situation even worse! You see this girl every. single. day!"

I scratched my head and bit my bottom lip as thought before I spoke.

"Look babe, swear I won't speak to that woman again, if it ain't about business or something that contains work I'll keep my mouth closed! I stepped out my boundaries and went too far, I know that and I'm Sorry, that's all I can say if you can't accept that then this relationship is in your hands, you can stay leave whatever it's up to you so what you want to do?"

"I don't know! I don't know what you're up to anymore, you stomp on my heart then expect it to be fixed with an apology that not how things work. I do want to be with you I don't talk to any other niggas, I don't fuck em I don't even like niggas pictures on Instagram," she said as tears slowly streamed down her beautiful face as her voice began cracking, she continued to speak "I feel stupid and I know them hoes are laughing at me cause I'm with a man that's supposed to be mines but steady flirting and talking to these bitches. What the point? What's the point of having a loyal woman on your side when you entertain and give them girl's time of day."

Seeing my woman cry makes me weak especially when I'm the source of her tears, I glanced up and watched her weep and felt unpleasant about the situation that I put our relationship in; I scooted to the front side of the bed an sat next to her then I wiped the tears off her face; with a soft touch I turned her face towards mines and I looked in her glossy eyes

"Babe, look at me, There's no other woman that can take your place."

I said kissing her soft lips, "This man sitting next to you loves you, I can't picture myself with anybody else but you, I'm sorry babe"

I kissed her lips some more then stared in her

eyes before asking her if she loved me.

She nodded her head, "You know I do Michael you just..."

(Makeup Sex)

I interrupted her and kissed the side of her neck with my full juicy lips, I kissed under her neck then made my way to the collar bone, I rubbed my wet tongue across her throat then ran it upward towards the right ear lobe. I sucked on her ear lobe as she slid her tongue across her lips and moaned softly. I caressed her body tightly as I kicked my shoes so I could get comfortable enough to lay in the bed, her stomach was flat with a few stretch Marks she was blessed with from giving birth to our child, I ducked my body low between her legs then began to Circle my tongue around her belly button, after my tongue ran laps around her stomach I ran it down the pelvis and licked across her panty line, her moans grew more intense as I teased the fuck out of her. I licked down her inner thighs and gently bit my way up towards the pussy.

Aggressively I slid the panties down then filled my mouth with saliva as my lips attach to her clitoris, I sucked and smack my tongue against her clit back and fourth constantly at a mild pace. Her pussy tasted fresh as Fiji water and had a mouth-watering scent. I licked and licked the clit as I sucked at the same time without changing my motions; I stuck my right index and middle finger inside her juicy vagina and arch them with the palm upwards to rub the roof of the pussy. I kept my tongue moving as my fingers were moisturized from stroking her G spot. After a couple of minutes her legs got stiff as she began to breathe heavily and call out

"Ohhhhhhhh Ohh shit ooolll!" She palmed the back of my head an smushed my face all in her pussy push her toes off the mattress to fuck my mouth, saliva leak down my chin an dripped into her ass crack flowing onto the sheets leaving wet spots. I shook my face in between her legs while I remained smacking the clit with my tongue and tickling her spot, in seconds she gripped tighter on the back of my head and dug her nail in my neck, she got a hand full of sheets with the opposite hand and screamed

"I'm CUMMMINGGGGG, Ohh what the fuckkkkk"

She let go of my head and grip the edge of the mattress as she came on my lips, I kept on sucking and licking the clit until every bone in her body gets flimsy. She pushed my forehead as she crawled backwards to detach my face from her Vagina , she was breathing like she ran a hundred miles and the expression on her face gave me a hint she was craving the dick, she pulled my shirt from the collar to bring me up to give her a kiss. In the midst of our tongues tying like shoe strings she reached down to unbuckle my pants, I removed my pants and boxer briefs then threw my shirt onto the floor, my 8 inch black dick was hard as a hammer handle and I was ready to plunge into Lisa who was on her back with her legs spread open across the bed! She moaned as I put the head of my dick inside her

"Mmmmmm damn babe" she said slowly as I pushed every inch far in. Her pussy was warm, slippery and tight the walls firmly took a grip of my dick. I got hold of her ankles with the left palm then connect her legs together and pushed them back towards her face, I threw my hips in her to send a perfect stroke. In and out, in and out. I dug into her like a shovel, our skin smacking together; she moaned as I talked shit,

"This is my pussy, this is my mothafuckin pussy" Im stroking and stroking, penetrating the pussy "You love this dick? you love this dick?"

"It's yours, it yours baby" she wailed as I continued dipping my hard dick in her juices. I can tell she was loving ever bit of this. I let go of her ankles to open her legs wide, I held her left ankle and let the right leg free just to spread them apart, with the free right hand I wrapped my palm around her throat to choke her as I pounded the pussy. Her eyes were closed tightly as she moaned at the top of her lungs. I'm bashing and bashing her insides non-stop giving her all my energy

"I LOVE YOU, I LOVE YOU MIKE OHHH MY GOD I LOVE YOU!!!" she yelled

"I LOVE YOU TOO BABE, MMMM GIVE ME THAT FUCKIN PUSSY"

"FUCK ME FUCK ME, OH HERE I CUM HERE I CUM, HERE I CUM" She announced!

I continued to stroke the same spot so she didn't lose her orgasm, in and out, here body stiffed

"I'M CUMMMINGGGGG OHH GOOOOOD"

I push my dick deep inside if her and held it in her to make her release a heart stopping nut, I pulled my penis out then went low to wrap my lips around her sensitive clitoris to have her cum again, I slid my tongue back and forth multiple times and in less then a minute she came.

"Stop Stop Stop" she said as she crawl back I kept on licking, with a mouth full of pussy I said

"What's the magic words?"

She had both hands on my forehead trying to push my head back

"I love you I love you I love you."

I glanced up at her and smiled. "Love you too now turn around."

She got into position on the right side of the bed with her ass up and her feet dangling of the edge, her ass was brown, round and soft like some delicious butter rolls,

I got behind her an reached for her left shoulder as I plunged my dick in her vagina again. While I stood on my feet I yanked on her shoulder to pull her ass into my waist punching my dick inside her.

"Yes yes Ohhhhh"

She's screaming gradually while I massaged her walls with my penis. I aggressively held her chin and push down on her spine to arch her back, the pussy felt like a high like no other and the fact that it was loyal pussy made the sex 10x better. I'm stroking her looking down and watching her take this dick thinking to myself

"I love this woman, I can't fuck this up"

She threw the ass at me with force; accidentally my thoughts came out quickly.

"Mmmmmmm I love you babe"

Stroking, stroking our bodies banged against each other.

I pulled my dick out the pussy then laid in the middle of the bed

"I want you to sit on it"

She didn't say any words, stood over me an squat down sliding slowly down the chocolate stick. I grabbed her ass from the side as she hopped up and down. I plant my feet down and used the mattress to lift my hips up every time she drop-down. Her titties bounced in my face, while I smacked her ass.

"I'm bout to cum," she said throwing her head back and riding me like a raging bull!

"Cum on this dick cum on this dick I want you to nut with me!" I called out.

"Here I cum here I cum."

As she screamed I felt the nut shoot right up my dick, and at the same time we both let loose, I held her body down

"Ahhhhhhhhhhhh!!!!" I said as I released the nut inside her pussy.

"Ohhhhhhhh fuck fuckkkkk" she moaned as her cum leak onto my dick. After the breathtaking nut, I kept my dick in her and she laid on my chest, I kissed her forehead then told her I loved her.

12. ANONYMOUS

It has been way too long and the guilt of not yet finishing this story is getting to me. I've been writing but I'm very busy. Being a hard-working family man, 24 hours a day simply isn't enough. Shit, I barely sleep. But finally I'm feeling relaxed on this warm Sunday evening. The sound of Jill Scott flows throughout my cozy townhome as candlelight dances off of the walls. Sitting at my desk, I finally type, "The End."

Overwhelmed with satisfaction, I exhale a sigh of a relief. With a half-smile, I shut my laptop and turn to head toward the couch.

ding

My iPhone alerts me to a new message. I told myself that I would be done handling business for the day, but of course, I reach for it anyway and read...

"I always wonder what sex with you would be like."

Oh... I had no idea who this mysterious person could be.

"I got a new phone. Who's this?" I lie, knowing damn well I've had this phone for almost a year.

"Good. I ain't telling you! 😝 "

Immediately a new story idea came to mind.

"Anonymous. This should be a good story lol." I reply.

"Good idea." My admirer sent a winking face.

Although Anonymous will turn out to be an amazing story, I am skeptical. I question this woman, as I need a hint as to who she could be.

"So how do I know you?"

"In a lot of ways."

Now I'm really confused. "How did you get my number?" I ask.

"You gave it to me."

"When? Where?"

"A couple of months ago on IG." She gives a slight smile via emoji.

Plenty of women slide in my DMs each week. Or I'm sliding in theirs so I still don't have a clue. I don't want to seem like I'm in every woman's messages so again, I lie. "I haven't given my number out on IG in a while." Meanwhile, I got @byeamber's number just a few hours ago. I chuckle to myself.

"Yeah yeah," she replies. Followed by another emoji. This time I'm getting the side eye. She knows what's up.

"What's your name on IG?" I ask fishing for hints.

"Really? I'm not giving you that." I pause the conversation for a minute.

"Ya stories make me horny." She chimes back in.

"Well thanks for reading. Is that why you wonder what sex with me would be like?" I grin as I press send.

"No. I just know it would be awesome."

"We shall see though."

"Can I be blindfolded? I don't want to know who you are lol." I ask. This should be interesting.

"How would that work?"

"Send me your address. When I get there, I'll text you. By the time you get to me, I'll be blindfolded and ready to be escorted to wherever you want to fuck me." I explain.

"Oh huhhhh."

"Damn, you're sexy and crazy."

"Well thank you. We'll make my next story."

"I don't wanna be disappointed. Are you as good as you write?" She questions my sexual performance.

"You'll have to find out for yourself." One thing to note about me is that I am very confident. I aim to please and I do so successfully. I go above and beyond to make sure that I shake a woman's soul. But I will be damned if I let her know that ahead of time.

"Most stories are from experience though." I appease her a bit.

"So….What happens at the end of our story?" she asks.

I raise an eyebrow. "You'll take me to my car and that's it. No strings attached."

"Naw lol. I guarantee you'll want to take that blindfold off."

"I guarantee that I won't. How do you figure that?"

"Cause I know." She replies quickly and with certainty.

"Oh, would you want me to?"
"Yes. Wouldn't you want to? Wouldn't you be curious?"

"Possibly. So when will this Anonymous story begin?" I finally ask. I'm beginning to get a little tired of this game.

"5809 Referral Lane, 15555. Be here in an hour."

"Now. Oh ok lol. I'll text you when I'm outside."

I stand up and pace back and forth a few times in disbelief, although I admit I'm a bit excited. This requires a call to my closest friend. The phone rang twice before he answers.

"What up bro?"

"Dawg, you're not going to believe what just happened."

"What happened bro?"

"Man, I got a text from this random chick wanting to know what my sex is about. I'm not sure if I want to slide over there or not."

"You're not sure if you want to slide over there or not? She might be bad for real and you'll never know unless you go over there."

"Man, you're a dog. You don't pass up any opportunities." I said laughing.

"Damn skippy. And if she's ugly just run for your life."

"I won't be able to see her until we're done fucking."

"What you mean?" He asks with confusion.

"I told her that I'll wear a blindfold to her house."

"Bruh. You have lost your mind. I would at least want to see what that's hitting for first."

"And where's the fun in that? I don't come up with all of these stories by erring on the side of caution. I'm wearing that blindfold." I chuckle. "I really called you to send you her address. If you don't hear from me for a few days you know what's up."

"Alright . Send that address to me one time with your paranoid ass."

"Man shut up, I'm about to send it now."

I hang up with him and laugh at myself as I text the address. "What am I about to get myself into?"

Before I know it, I'm cruising through the city in my black on black Impala; blindly following my GPS to this woman's house as PartyNextDoor plays distantly in the background. My thoughts are much louder though. They're interrupted by my GPS, "Arrived."

She lives in a middleclass neighborhood and her house just so happens to be behind the high school from which I graduated. There is a white picket fence, a decent sized yard with a giant tree, leaves fallen everywhere, a nice little walkway and a few steps leading up to a covered porch. (WHITE DOORS, APT 2½) After briefly peeping the scenery, I reach for my phone and text Ms. Anonymous. "Hey love I'm outside"

"Another ten minutes and you would have missed me." She replies quickly.

"Well I made it." I reply confused since she initiated this meeting.

"Okay, I have rules since you want to be kinky."

I raise an eyebrow and reply, "Lol rules?"

"I will not speak to you. The only thing you will hear coming from me are moans. When you come into my house, take off every single article of clothing and sit in the chair to the right of the doorway. I will allow you to speak. But only when you feel pleasure."

"Okay, anything else?"
"Yes, put your blind fold on now. Make sure that it's secured with nothing visible. I will be out to get you in three minutes."
"Okay." I remove the keys from the ignition and put them in my pocket along with my phone. I place the blindfold over my eyes and tighten the strings in the back so that it is secure to my head. I can't see a damn thing. Feeling a bit of angst in the pit of my stomach, I take a deep breath and exhale. Let the games begin.

In what I'm sure was exactly three minutes, she opens my car door. She reaches in to check the security of my blindfold. Then surprisingly, she gives me a slightly gentle, but lingering kiss. She smells amazing... and sweet. A bit familiar, but I can't pinpoint the scent. After just a moment, she tugs lightly on my shirt. I bite my lip and step out slowly. She interlocks her arm with mine and guides me through the yard, up the steps and through the doorway.

I hear the door shut softly behind me. I guess that's my cue. I kick off my shoes and slide my socks off while simultaneously removing my jean jacket and hoodie. I slowly lift my t-shirt over my head being careful not to shift the blindfold from my eyes. I slow down a little as I can feel her watching me. I unbuckle my belt and drop my pants. I pause for a moment before pulling my boxer briefs down. I'm sure by now she's in awe at what is standing in front of her. I'm entirely exposed and at her mercy.

The air smells spicy and there's a slight chill. All of a sudden, her heels and the sound of a chair sliding across the floor approach from behind. The chair hits the back of my calves, forcing me to take a seat. I take in a deep breath as that sweet, familiar smell crosses my nose again. She yanks both of my arms behind the chair and slaps handcuffs around each wrist. Instantly I'm aroused and standing at attention. "You didn't mention handcuffs."

She ignores me and runs her finger across my shoulders, making her way down my arm. She steps around to reach my thigh and kneels in front of me. Now gripping my thighs, she whispers, "Damn it's thick AND long… mmmm just looking makes my mouth water." Feeling her warm breath on my dick gives me chills. She grabs my shaft and begins to stroke.

I somehow mutter, "You broke a rule. You said..." and before I can finish the sentence her wet mouth swallows me whole. "Ohhh shiiiit...." I say as my toes curl uncontrollably. She's sucking and twisting her wrists, stroking my dick at a mild pace. I feel her hair bounce on my abs every time she takes the dick down. She held and pushed my dick toward my stomach, continuing to stroke. She then spits on my balls and wiggles her tongue back and forth across them. The more intense the feeling, the tighter the cuffs get as I swarm in the chair. "Ohhh fuck fuck fuck" I wailed. I ball my fists up unsure of how much more I can take without exploding. I can barely control myself. This woman is snatching my soul.

She stops licking for a second. I sigh with relief. I can't go out like this. Suddenly she wraps her mouth around my balls, licking and humming on them, causing my testicles to vibrate. Chills run through me and my legs stiffen as I let out a long moan. "Oh what the fuck, what the fuck are you doing to me?"

She doesn't say anything, but lets out a sexy moan and a little giggle as she continues to lick, suck and hum while beating my dick all in the same act. She knows what she's doing. And at this very moment, I feel like her sex slave. She has full control of my mind, body and feelings.

Just before I was ready to explode all in her mouth, she stops and lets me go. I suddenly become aware of the wet mess she's left all over my lap. My muscles begin to loosen as I lose the buildup that was about to be sliding down her throat. Her heels click across the floor and away from me again and she returns quickly with yet another surprise. Headphones. It doesn't take long for me to realize that I'm listening to a threesome. My senses go insane. I can hear two women moaning as the man talks his shit.

"Eat her fucking pussy and take this dick," he demands as he fucks her at a hard, but steady tempo. My imagination runs wild. In my mind I see a man throwing dick at a woman from behind; Her ass clapping with every stroke and her face all in the pussy of another woman who's trying to run from the head, but can't because she's propped up on a couch wide open. Ecstasy everywhere.

Speaking of ecstasy, it's been at least two minutes since the Anonymous woman touched me. What the fuck is going on? I'm way too exposed for this shit. I feel like I'm in a spotlight. She is psychologically and sexually manipulating me, and I don't think my mind has ever been this scattered. Where did she go? What is she doing? This woman is crazy as fuck, but that head was on point. I can't wait to see who she is. I might have to wife this bitch.

My thoughts are again interrupted and refocused on what is playing in my ears. "Open that mouth and stick your tongue out." He orders. "Cum in my mouth, Daddy." She says as the man moans and groan. The audio fades to silences. Five minutes go by and nothing. Not a sound and no Ms. Anonymous.

"Yo what the hell are you doing?" I say attempting to get a response out of her. I hear nothing. My patience is running short, and my dick has gotten soft. I think I'm starting to come to my senses as I sit here naked and handcuffed with a blindfold over my eyes. I've had enough. "Yo I quit. I'm done. I'm getting out of these cuffs." I exclaim as I struggle to even twist and turn my wrists.

As I actually start putting forth effort to escape, I feel a cold sensation on my chest. I jump and take the chair in the air with me as if I had been shocked. "OH SHIT!" I screamed as my heart pounds damn near out my chest. She removes the headphones and continues to rub the ice across my chest while she stands behind me, kissing and biting my neck. In no time my dick is right back at attention. The water from the ice melting rolls down my chest and stomach to my dick and balls. Her kisses are warm and she smells like Dove soap. I presume she had taken a shower in the time she had left me alone.

I now feel her lips with an ice cube between them; travelling slowly up my neck toward the back of my left ear lobe. "Damn baby." I moaned as the melting ice runs down my back. "You got me." She steps in front of me and kisses my lips then shoves her tongue in my mouth to transfer the ice from her lips to mine. She steps around and aggressively pulls the handcuffs back just enough to deliver a slight pain in my wrists.

click *click*

The left cuff swings open, then the right. Ms. Anonymous grabs my dick with a firm grip. She yanks it, forcing me to stand and start walking forward. She guides me through her house like a dog on a leash, and escorting me up the stairs to her bedroom. It's warm and smells like incense. This aroma, again is very familiar.

She kisses me on my lips then she takes her hands and presses upon my chest commanding me to fall back. I can feel the mattress on the back of my knees so I fall back. She starts guiding me to scoot back and then tells me to stop. I can feel the pillow at the top of my head.

I feel the mattress start to sink in as she climbs over top of my upper body then sink in some more as she eases her way up to my head, she then squats down on my face. She presses her wet pussy against my lips I open my mouth and stick my tongue out using it to find her clit. I suck her clit gently and kiss it like I missed it once I found it.

"Ow yes," she wails as I

lick and lick in a steady mild pace I'm eating her sweet pussy like it was my last meal. At this moment, I feel like I have gained control of the show. Her juices flow down my mouth, down my chin like a warm water, her moans get louder

"Oh yes, yes mmhm yes!"

Licking and sucking with no intention of stopping I was craving for her to cum in my mouth

"Oh yes Aron yes!" She continues as she grinds her pussy against my mouth literally fucking the shit out my face.

"Yes yes mmhm eat that pussy, eat that fucking pussy!" She demands in sexy soft tone.

I make an attempt to recognize the voice as she moans and blur out my name but I still have no clue who she is. She grabs the back of my head and smashes it into her delicious pussy; smearing my face all in it. I keep on licking as she puts an effort in to gain control back but I can't let her. I reach up grabbing her by the waist pulling her off of my face. I ease my body from under her still keeping my blindfold on I stood up "lay down on your back" I demand.

"Okay," she replies with no hesitation I can hear her get in position and stop. I reach out and used my hands to guide me to her body. I reach down and can feel her ankles, I grab both and attach her legs together placing them vertically in the air, I then push her legs back toward her face and hold them with my left hand.

"Oh fuck!" She let out right before I dive face first in her wet pussy with no scuba gear. I stick my long thick tongue out and stroke her pussy fully starting from the bottom to the top then I stick it in between the lips, dig my tongue inside her pussy and forcing her to fuck my face again; dipping in and out

"Ohh fuck!" She dramatically wails once more as her body lightly quivers.

I pull my tongue out, spread her legs apart then I place my hands below her pelvis all in the same act that I spread the pussy lips apart to give me more access to lick her aroused clit. I wrap my lips around it then I begin to suck the soul out of her, stiffing my tongue I slide the tip of it up and down, back and forward. I feel her body drift back as she continues to moan, I feel her body arch and her legs continue to shake.

"Oh yes, keep going keep going I'm about to cum!"

My tongue moves like I had Energizer batteries in it, if you ask me I think my tongue performs greater than a vibrator. I keep eating her pussy I can feel her grabbing the sheets, her legs start to tighten up around my head.

"Ohhhh lord yes oh my gosh yessss!" She screams from the top of her lungs while she pulls my face deeper in pussy as she squeezes my head with her thighs.

I can hear her breathing heavy, I smile and proudly ask, "Is this what you expected?"

She didn't answer I feel the bed sink in then I hear her step away from the bed; I lay in the middle of the bed still blind I reach back for a pillow, I place the pillow under my head

Not even a minute passes I heard her walk toward then I feel her crawl in. She grabs hold of my dick firmly and I feel something drip down the tip, she starts stroking my hard dick up and down, twisting like she was in pottery class then I feel her climb over top of me as her hand remains on the root of my dick. She introduces my dick inside her warm wet pussy and slowly slides down my dick. I can hear her breathing change as she eases down inch by inch, she lets out a soft moan when she finally has all eight inches of my hard dick inside her.

She places her hand on my chest then bounces on my dick at a slow pace, the pussy is tightly squeezing my dick creating an amazing friction, I grab her soft ass then I jam my dick farther up in her as she comes down on it.

"Mmhmm that pussy wet for me?" I say as she bounces up and down on the dick while I continue to push it all deep inside her pussy. I feel her grasping tighter on my chest as she remains to moan every second she comes down on it.

I pull her towards me chest to chest and wrap my arms around her lower back then I bend my knee and place my feet flat on the bed for a firm stroke. Using my waist I lift up and stroke upwardly as I forcefully push her lower body deeper on my dick, she moans louder as I dig my dick inside her greatness.

"Fuck fuck fuck!" She wails cursing a storm

My goal is to please I felt myself about to cum so I slow the stroke down to prevent myself from cumming too early; I damn near almost have to stop because the pussy is that fucking good.

"Let me get on top, matter fact get up and turn around" I demand.

She slowly gets up then scoots her ass back on my dick for me. I push her back in causing her to arch her back and lay her chest on the bed. I stand behind her with my knees on the bed, I plug my dick in her then begin to stroke her slowly.

"Damn this feels good," I say pushing every inch in her pussy and holding it down for a few second

"Oh my gosh oh my gosh!" She screams as I hear a banging noise on the mattress. I pull out then hold the dick down in her for a few more seconds

"Oh my Gosh I love this fucking dick Aron."

I pull her upper body up from the bed to my chest, guiding my right hand up body grabbing a hand full of her breast before I make my way to her neck and choke her by the throat

"Now I got to punish you for breaking the rules!" I say as I began penetrating with aggression from behind, I feel her thighs vibrating as I stroke the pussy

"Ow yes! Yes Aron! Yes Aron!" She wails my name again. This woman is very experienced. She throws her ass back as I deliver each stroke, with the free hand I stick my thumb in my mouth to soak it with saliva then I slowly insert it in her butt.

In a few strokes her whole body weakens. "I'm about to cum again baby I'm about to cum" she announces.

I keep on throwing the dick in her and jamming my thumb deeper in her anus.

"Ohh shit" she wails as she punches down on the mattress.

I grip tighter on her neck and stroke with passion and force as sweat drips from my forehead. "Cum on my dick"

I feel myself about to cum as well as moans. "I'm cumminggg!" She screams out loud as her body shakes like a seizure.

I push the dick in the pussy and hold it down in her pussy as she melts all over it.

"Keep going keep going baby I want you to cum too." I slowly stroke from the back as she continues to moan, the nut rushes from my testicle, I pull my dick out and bust on her back.

"Mmhmmmm damn yo" I collapse and lay next to her as I breath massively. "So what's next" I'm the first to break the silence.

"Take your blindfold off"

"Help me it's kinda tight"

She unwraps it then I get a good glance at her it was...

Made in the USA
Middletown, DE
27 March 2022